THE
ROBERT OLEN BUTLER
PRIZE STORIES

2007

THE
ROBERT OLEN BUTLER
PRIZE STORIES

2007

)•)

DEL SOL PRESS

WASHINGTON, D.C.

The Robert Olen Butler Prize Stories 2007

DEL SOL PRESS, WASHINGTON, D.C.

HTTP://WEBDELSOL.COM/DSP

PAPER ISBN: 978-0-9791501-6-6

FIRST EDITION

COVER PHOTOGRAPH:
© PHOTOGRAPHER: BRIAN CHASE | AGENCY: DREAMSTIME.COM

COVER DESIGN BY ANDER MONSON

INTERIOR DESIGN BY ANDER MONSON

CONTEST COORDINATION IN 2006-2007 BY JACOB POWERS

Publication by Del Sol Press/Web del Sol Association, a not-for-profit corporation under section 501 (c) (3) of the United States Internal Revenue Code.

❧ *Contents* ❧

The 2007 Prize Winner

❧ *Jasmine, Washing the Hair of Pearsa* ❧

VALERIE HURLEY

I WAS EXPECTED TO ARRIVE IN THE WORLD ON APRIL 2, 1957, but two weeks later I hadn't arrived, nor two months later, nor two years later. My condition was a rare medical phenomenon in human parturition that would later be written up in textbooks, but at the time I was beginning to wonder if I was imagining my life as a fetus. My mother was concealing me in her womb. Perhaps she was afraid my eyes would be green and almond-shaped, like the parish priest's?

Jasmine lived on donut fat, greasy chicken, and the crisp, blue light of alcohol. The smell of rolls baking in the oven, or meat roasting, or tomato sauce simmering on the stove was unknown to us, for my mother was a con-noisseur of delicatessen food—cole slaw, Oreos, and lukewarm French fries. She inhaled gales of hairspray. She drank quarts of champagne. On this diet I might have managed for nine months, but after two years in her uterus, I had become a bloated, froglike creature with puffy muscles, waterlogged ears, and blurry eyesight. As I whiled away my time in the womb, I imag-ined Jasmine putting on "The Tennessee Waltz," poking a flower behind her ear and dancing around the rooms. Her apartment was behind her beauty parlor, and I could hear the tapping of her high heels on the linoleum floors, with the milky scent of permanent wave solution drifting down the narrow hallway.

My mother liked to sit under the Big Dipper. This was the closest she ever got to questioning anything. She was a great believer in murk and ambi-guity and the assurance that nothing—like right and wrong—was absolute. She read about Sigmund Freud in the set of thin encyclopedias she pur-chased at the A & P and kept a picture of him, cut out of the *Ladies' Home Journal*, taped to the bathroom wall. "If I cannot move heaven, I will stir up the underworld," she loved to say, quoting the great man.

She whispered her sins to Father McCrory in the confessional on Saturday afternoons, received the communion wafer from him on Sunday mornings, and settled into a creaky bed with him on Wednesday afternoons. The bed was in an old farmhouse on Buzzards Bay surrounded by swamps full of yellow iris and red-winged blackbirds. I loved to listen to the muffled sound of the birds singing.

"I never could resist the forbidden," Jasmine said to Father McCrory one Wednesday. "When I was little, I loved to crawl under the house and have a cigarette and a little gin and lemonade. There's something so tantalizing about forbidden merchandise!" With this she grabbed him and had him giggling like a ten-year-old.

The longer I stayed in her womb, the more moralistic I became. Why wasn't my mother like the other women in the neighborhood, the housewives she gossiped with as she cut and curled and bleached their hair? Shouldn't she be cooking, ironing, and washing clothes? Shouldn't he be visiting his parishioners? I'd lie between them in bed, dreaming of skipping, playing hopscotch, and swinging from trees—vague desires for things I knew nothing about. My biggest problem was that I never wanted to inconvenience my mother.

The janitor at the church was also fond of Jasmine and arrived every Monday with flower arrangements from the altar. Lilies, slightly browned at the edges, or bunches of spidery carnations. She hugged him—or we all hugged—rather intensely, I thought, and he took a beer out of the refrigerator and told her his woes as she sat plucking the curlers out of her hair.

She never, as far as I could tell, noticed me or thought about me. Sometimes I'd find the courage to thump on her uterus, and she'd say, "Oh, my lumbago!" In the mornings, she dyed, cut and curled women's hair, and in the afternoons, she shopped for clothes or sat by the window, drinking champagne.

If it were not for my mother's wardrobe—closets full of ostrich feather belts, flower-laden straw hats, silk dresses, curly lamb coats and satin bed jackets—I might still be residing in her uterus. Her clothes irritated me because they subjected both of us to her lover's effusive compliments, interminable conversations with saleswomen in stores, and chatty deliberations in front of the mirror each morning. The day she purchased four pairs of shoes for her two little feet, I finally got angry enough to begin the big move from my mother's warm uterus into her cool arms. And so, on a Wednesday in May, with the bullfrogs signing out their mating calls, two years, ten months, and twenty-three days after my conception, I decided it was time to be born.

"Well, I'll be darned!" Father McCrory exclaimed. I lay on the farmhouse bed, fat and weak, my skin rumpled and yellowish, my vision dim, my blonde hair long and bedraggled as they hovered above me, totally stupefied. For better or worse, there they were: my mommy and daddy.

🐚 🐚

Jasmine and Father McCrory did not always get along. He occasionally showed signs of becoming conscience-stricken, which was not a trait Jasmine admired in a man. She always managed to get him settled back into the relationship, but it seemed obvious that his Wednesdays with Jasmine were not as free of care as they once had been. One day, he tried to interest her in a more innocent activity. Like what? she asked. Could they possibly go across the river to Fairhaven and do errands together on Saturdays?

"Of course, lovey," Jasmine said with an icy smile. She made it a point never to disagree with a man, but it didn't seem likely they'd be doing errands together on Saturdays since Jasmine didn't do errands but fully believed that's what children were for. This was the point at which I started to do Father McCrory's errands, as well as our own. I was around eleven at the time, with Jasmine chomping at the bit until she could yank me out of school and get me working full-time at the salon, so off I went each Saturday to the shoemaker and the pharmacy and the Chinese laundry and the gas company while Jasmine and Father McCrory drove off in the church's black Packard to a distant town to share a foamy beer.

Father McCrory and I looked at each other with a sense of commiseration, and a sort of unspoken alliance formed between us as Jasmine's lapdogs. I never had the feeling he considered me his daughter. Such yokage would be clearly immoral, and I could see it was a thought that rarely if ever entered the good priest's head—but I knew he liked me, and I liked him. To both of us, life without Jasmine was unimaginable.

I dreamed of having my hair done in the Mane Attraction, and everyone turning to admire me as I walked into the classroom. Girls arrived in school with their hair lovingly braided, or wound up in velvet ribbons. I would have liked it if Jasmine had decided to peroxide my hair or fix it with millions of pin-curls, making me, if not pretty, at least noticeable in some way—but her beauty salon, she had made it clear, was not for the likes of me.

Nor did her interest in clothes extend to my own wardrobe. Most of my clothes came from the Salvation Army Hurricane Relief bin behind the dumpster at St. Columbine's Church. I envied my schoolmates who arrived in dresses starched and ironed with bows on their socks and shoes to match. But Jasmine's rule was that a child was entitled to only eight pairs of shoes during childhood, and I, at age eleven, was already on my seventh pair. Any child with more than eight pairs of shoes to her credit was clearly a spoiled child, and she had announced rather early on that no child of hers would be spoiled.

On Sundays, Jasmine and I attended Mass together, and I had a chance to hear Father McCrory declaim from the pulpit. He was a tall, portly man with a shy smile and the worried, startled expression of a fish, and his faith in God was genuine enough to arouse his sleepy flock. I could see that his sins stood him in good stead and fulfilled a necessity in his life—for his deep humility was nearly enchanting, and nothing can sour a roomful of sinners faster than someone in their midst who is not engaged in sinning. We could all see that Father McCrory was not branches above us like the Monsignor in his scarlet hat.

But his career, I knew, rested on my invisibility. A girl like me with haywire blonde hair and sad poodle eyes could topple an empire it had taken him several decades to build. Surely God could not have intended that?

He had his honest moments, though—never about his surprise fatherhood but occasionally about his dangerous propensity to climb into bed with the gardenia-flavored Jasmine. One day, when I was reading about the fascinating way octopi ensnare their prey with their tough, parrot-like beaks, I heard his voice waffling through the wallboard. "I should cast away the priesthood and go away disgraced," he said.

"Go away where?" Jasmine asked.

"Into Limbo, with the unbaptized."

"Limbo?"

"Where there's never any chance of ever seeing God."

"Whatever for?" Jasmine asked.

"For my unrepentance."

"Adam and Eve were unrepentant, too, but if it wasn't for them, we wouldn't be sitting here having this talk," Jasmine said calmly. A long pause ensued, and even through the wall, I could tell that the matter was settled.

"And then there is an awful shortage of priests," Father McCrory declared.

In the rooms behind the beauty parlor, I became the adult who seems to materialize in such situations—a dreamy, quiet child who prepared dinner every night, washed the dishes, trekked to the Laundromat, and faithfully squeezed out lettuce juice each night to treat my mother's insomnia. For years, I tended to her and a coterie of admirers until finally I fell in love with bees and wandered weakly out into my own life—but never into my own relationships. It appeared that I could only relate to my mother.

"Did Father McCrory mean something special to you?" I asked Jasmine the day I moved out of our apartment.

"Oh yes," she said. "He's the best priest on the planet, other than the Pope."

"I mean personally."

"Personally? Why, what are you suggesting, Jessica? You naughty girl!"

"Just that I was wondering if you ever loved him."

"Why, of course I loved him. Who wouldn't love such a holy man who's given his life to God? A man who loves everyone, and everyone loves him."

"But wouldn't you say there was something special between you?" I asked.

"Of course I would! He's the most understanding confessor I've ever encountered in all my thirty-nine years."

I wondered how Jasmine could be thirty-nine when I was thirty-two, but as usual, I said nothing. Extracting any kind of information from her always made me feel deficient in some way. Her pupils—enlarged with jimson weed—would bore into me, suggesting that perhaps we could talk about something more pleasant. Her ice-blue eyes would boil up, she'd adjust the flower in her hair, her little foot would begin to tap on the floor, and these mannerisms, coupled with a gentle look of puzzlement, would steer me toward a fresh subject.

Jasmine's life was chock-full of pleasantries, which is why, perhaps, she was attracted to Freud, that smasher of all that seemed to be. A real encounter with such a man would send her running—but a suggestion of his dark, probing brilliance as she brushed her teeth in the morning seemed to fortify her in some way, and added immeasurably to her cheerful moods.

❧ ❦

When I was thirty-five, I said to my mother, "There's a man in my life. He has a thousand hives up near Buttonwood Park."

"Hives?" she said. "He has hives?"

"He's a beekeeper. Like me."

"You have the most gorgeous bedroom eyes, lovey. If only you knew how to use them."

Jasmine was dressed in a pair of orange satin pedal-pushers, a lacy lime-green blouse, alligator shoes, a ratty mink collar, and a long strand of purple pop-it beads. I kept a baseball bat in the closet for intruders, and sometimes I imagined taking it and battering to a pulp every glove, necklace, dress, gown, shoe, purse, and negligee Jasmine owned. But would I actually resist an intruder, or was intrusion an impossible state for me?

"Jasmine," I said, "we need to settle some of our grievances. You used to mail me postcards from Florida. You said you'd send for me and we'd go scuba diving and have ice cream sundaes for breakfast."

She grinned and clasped her hands together. "Oh yes! What fun!"

"But it *wasn't* fun, Jasmine, because it was only an idea. You never sent for me."

Patches of sunlight were fluttering on the floor of my little house. The gentle scent of lilacs was streaming through the rooms. I was determined at last to give her a piece of my mind as she sat at my red Formica table with a gardenia in her hair and a choker of paste pearls around her neck. She took out her compact and coated her lips an evil shade of maroon. Then she sighed, surveying the rings on her fingers—rhinestones and amethysts and peridots from Woolworth's—and said, "Something's missing in this house. Some Y chromosomes."

I sat down across from her and stared into her blue eyes. She was not domestic, soothing, comforting, or nurturing, yet somehow men found her appealing. She always looked as though she were about to burst into an aria.

I stood up, drew in a deep breath and said, "The only thing I can remember you doing for me is reading *Civilization and its Discontents* out loud every Friday night." Even my insults had to be presented as compliments.

Feeling unburdened, as though I had actually *said* something, I went out into the yard and broke off one of the pink hydrangeas for her silver hair. I was no match for her, and I knew it. I hated conflict. I was a peacemaker who fought all skirmishes on my own internal turf. My loneliness, I decided, was like living inside an argument without an opponent. She never blamed me for her woes because she had no woes, and somehow I was hesitant to blame her for mine. I wanted to tell her how it was for me, but I did not have the words or even the thoughts to describe my life. I wanted to blame her for my deficiencies—but who could accuse this cheery little dancer of anything? She had worked hard to support us. She improved the lives of her clients, chattering merrily as she rolled their hair into mesh rollers or lovingly obliterated streaks of gray. She made men happy. She never nagged them, criticized them, or tried to change them. She was the perfect woman—a scented, flowery wisp content to simply be in their presence.

I went back into the house and closed all the blinds, as if to keep her in. I took the phone off the hook, and standing in front of the mirror, pinned the hydrangea into my hair. I knew so little about the beekeeper. Did he love flowers? Was he interested in my thoughts? Did he find me pretty? What would make him happy? Would his soft beeswax hands ever touch me? I went into the kitchen, sat down, and rested my bedroom eyes on Jasmine's small mischievous face.

"Jessica, let me wash your hair," she said.

I put my hand up and felt the soft flower collapsing under my fingers.

"What fun!" she said. "We'll wash your hair and get you ready for your beekeeper!" She had sprung out of the chair and was hurrying up the stairs, and I stood up and took my place by the sink and wondered what our footsteps would sound like, the beekeeper's and mine, tapping softly on the wooden stairs. Happy? Scared? It had been years since I had shared a deep emotion with another human being.

Her arms filled with towels, hair rollers, brushes, shampoo, and cream rinse, she appeared in the doorway.

"Jasmine," I said, "maybe it's time for our talk about the birds and the bees."

"Oh, I think not, darling," she said, flapping a terrycloth towel in the air and arranging her supplies in a circle on the table. Would a man ever call me darling? Or would such a word be too ornate for someone as plain as me? I stared at my face reflected out of the toaster, a crinkling rectangle of flesh split with crow's feet—even in the blurry chrome, an unmistakable virgin.

"Jasmine, when people of the opposite sex unite—do they actually become one?" I asked, remembering the experience of being one with her.

"One? I should say not!"

"What then?"

"What do they become?" She laid her jeweled hands out over the pink and blue rollers and gazed at me, as though she had never thought about it. "Like the flower and the bee," she said, "very natural, together for only an instant—sometimes in ecstasy, sometimes not—but always filled with longing and compelled to unite."

"Compelled to unite?"

"That's what makes it all so terribly exciting—that compulsion," she said.

"I seem to feel compelled *not* to unite."

"And do you know why? Men can't stand women with scruples. Curls! Mystery! Laughter! Perfume! That's what they're looking for. Not a woman who shops in thrift stores and smells like an upholstered chair."

I thought of the bee dances, the bees' way of indicating the locations and strengths of nectar sources. "But what exactly *is* it like, Jasmine, to have a man lie down on top of you and—"

"There's only a few ways of finding out such things, and asking your mother is probably the worst of them," she said.

"But I mean—is it enjoyable?"

"Jessica, my mother was a gypsy, and she never had much to say to me. But one piece of advice I will always remember."

I perked up, imagining a pie-baking grandmother who dressed in black, spoke Rumanian, kept beehives, and smelled of lavender. "What's that?"

"Don't tell all you know, even if it doesn't take long."

I leaned over the sink, my head feeling like a huge egg cupped in Jasmine's hands. The shampoo smelled of pineapple and gardenias, and I thought of the gardens in Florida where I had once dreamed of spending time with her. *Mother!* I wanted to call up to her through the silver streaming water, the glistening golden hair. *Mother!* She rinsed and rinsed my hair until it glittered like corn silk, the afternoon sun pouring through it, through the organdy curtain, shaking circles of gold onto her old hands. Suddenly she couldn't stop taking care of me. I felt the gates opening and my mother's love flooded out over me. "Pearsa," she whispered—or did I imagine it? Pearsa, the secret gypsy name whispered to the child at birth.

Dripping with water and blinking in the sun, I raised my head. She tossed a towel at me. Never quick enough for her, I dropped it, and it lay in a swirl of pink at my feet. I leaned over to pick it up, feeling my breasts large and dangling and my heart singing in rhythm with his. I saw his face before me, blissful and smiling. I shook out my wet hair and wrapped it gracefully in the towel, my elbows rising in the air like the wings of a swan. "What did you say, Mother?"

"*Mother!*" Jasmine yelped. "That makes me sound so *old.*"

Yet she seemed pleased.

As a child, I had imagined rivers boiling, lightning flashing behind her eyes, and in some place deep within her, where I could never find them, where she hid them from me, a heap of pearls. Now, sitting in my house, at my kitchen table, with the clock ticking and the rose mallows and sunflowers leaning against the window glass, I felt I could simply reach over and take the pearls. But it would be like stealing.

I could feel the beekeeper standing behind me as I said, "You never took care of me, Jasmine."

"No—but you take care of me, Jessica, and you do lovely at it. The young taking care of the old—isn't that as it should be?"

"We have to be taught how to love, or shown," I said. "Don't you think?"

"Oh yes—I certainly do, dearheart."

"That was something you never showed me," I said.

"Life doesn't owe us anything, other than a tumble down the birth canal. Don't expect anything, and you won't be disappointed."

"But you drank all that cheap champagne! You wouldn't admit you were pregnant with me. You hated being fat!"

"And take a look at you—a huge, strapping girl! Adversity always strengthens us, don't you know? You have your own house, and your life is filled with all those bees. I don't know if I could have pictured anything better for you."

"Why did you hang Freud's picture on the bathroom wall?"

"I felt strangely enchanted by Sigmund because his real name was Sigismund. He changed it in school. I find men who change their names fascinating, as though they're hiding something, and I always want to find out what it is. He smoked cigars and lived in Venice."

"Vienna, you mean?"

"Venice, Vienna. I always liked his eyes."

"You seem to almost enjoy being mean."

"You're too nice," she said. "You give too much and people take advantage of you."

I sighed. Getting angry at her was an exhausting undertaking. I thought of the tarantula-killer wasp stinging a huge spider and storing it in a drugged state by its egg. I thought of the nurse bees secreting food from their heads for the footless white grubs. Jasmine had none of the order and industry and naturalness of honeybees—but she had the venom and she wasn't afraid to use it.

As a child, I was wary of her. But I had made friends with Freud over the years, the dark picture on the bathroom wall splattered with toothpaste, the determination in his eyes never softening, his gaze always boring on toward truth. The neediness I felt for Jasmine I didn't want to feel for the beekeeper. People should love each other and want each other but not *need* each other, Jasmine had often said, and it was one bit of her wisdom I truly believed.

We kept our hives in Buttonwood Park. We worked side by side and sometimes talked, but it was always about bees, and he did most of the talking. All around us were bushes of honeysuckle in bloom and the big, glittering eyes of the drones. I wanted to reach out for him, but I knew I was not the kind of woman who could stretch a hand out and touch a man. And he himself was bashful.

Nothing was keeping us apart—yet it was impossible for me to imagine myself taking even a tiny step toward him. I had rarely taken a step toward anyone or anything, although I had finally dislodged myself from Jasmine's chambers and purchased a little house two miles distant from her beauty shop. Years of wishing, planning and indecisiveness preceded this move—but did I have years to spend on my move toward the beekeeper, or would I someday find myself dancing at his wedding? And who would I be dancing with?

Bees work solely on instinct and practicality and never have even the pettiest struggle with sin. If the queen needs to be killed while stuffed fatly into her cell, the murder is carried out with aplomb. I sometimes wished that my struggles were with right and wrong rather than with the demons of my own and Jasmine's design. Where were the rules? Where was the truth we lived by? Jasmine said she didn't believe in the Ten Commandments but in the Seven Laws of Noah, whatever they were. But in spite of what the church fathers thought, I had begun to realize that Father McCrory was lucky to feel love and the compulsion to unite—and to have acted upon it. Wasn't his receptivity to love a gift he gave back to God for his rich life?

Here I was being held back from the beekeeper not by the church or state—but by the twisted forces Freud had consecrated his life to. (His photograph was now posted on *my* bathroom wall.)

I watched a bee lay its two pairs of wings along its back. I listened to the sound of humming wings. I marveled at the queen placing a lump of beebread in the dry hollow of an old mouse nest, and eating from the honeypot as she sat upon her eggs. Had I dreamed up his beauty or was it real? Did we love each other—or was I imagining it?

We stood together one morning talking about the leaf-cutting bees who line their cells with abandoned snail shells. "I met your mother in the Laundromat," he said.

"It couldn't have been my mother. She's never been in a Laundromat."

"It was your mother, Jessica."

"You met Jasmine?"

"I was wearing my bee shirt, and she came over and started talking about her daughter who kept bees. She told me all about you."

"What about me?" I said.

"Mostly that you were into bees but you hadn't blossomed yet. You needed a man to draw you out."

Jasmine was the sort of woman who always had her fingers in the jampot. I felt the fury gathering in my legs and working its way up through me, and when it reached my eyes, I knew I'd cry and I wouldn't be able to stop. I pictured huge silvery tears splashing out from under my eyeglasses, all over the beekeeper. "What else did she say?" I asked.

He laughed. "Oh, she was very talkative. She told me all about your childhood, your interest in insects. She'd go after the little devils with a can of Raid, but you'd try to catch them in a glass and take them outside."

"Yes," I said. "I loved setting them free."

"She said she doesn't really know where you came from. She thinks the stork dropped you off."

"She knows where I came from," I said.

"I liked hearing her stories. I've always been curious about you. You're so quiet."

The tears never arrived, but the words did—and I could not believe what I was saying. I told him I had some money saved, and I wanted to take a trip to Vienna. Could he watch my hives for me until I returned? I wanted to discuss with someone other than Jasmine the tenderness I was beginning to feel for a man who, like me, loved the order of work, the tumble of eyes and fur and stinger, the buzzing, dancing, and humming of bees.

❧ ❦

I sat in Freud's office, now a small museum at Berggasse 19, knowing only one thing—that the brook knows how to find the river and the river the sea. Shelves along the walls held the Chinese Buddha, the marble horse, the falcon-headed Horus, the Assyrian winged bull, the bird deity, the

Egyptian cobra, the Roman citizen. The rooms were full of Oriental rugs, faded velvet cushions, antimacassars, flowered drapes. Sunlight wavered on the reds in the carpet, on the scarlet and fuchsia, the amethyst, the violet. Outside the window was a courtyard and garden, Vienna with its scraping trams and clopping horses, its Sacher tortes and Turkish coffee, its bureaucrats, its waltzing.

Each day I returned. A bowl of the orchids Freud had loved stood on a mahogany table. I told the caretakers that I was a student of Freud's, and I sat in the courtyard below, overgrown with lupine, roses, iris, date-palm, mockorange and glossy Viennese lilies. On a crumbling stone bench, I sat for hours. No one in the window above noticed me. I was invisible to other people except to the beekeeper who had spoken to me each morning and evening and looked at me warmly, his eyes glittering like a bride's through his net of white.

In the morning, I walked up from the Pension Pertschy on Habsburgergasse, climbed the stairs and stood by the door on the second floor marked with the brass plate *Prof. Dr. Freud*. With clattering keys, the door was unlocked, the birds sang in the locust trees, the smell of coffee drifted into the tile hallway.

I entered Freud's rooms, studying the figurines and the loose-leaf binder which enumerated each artifact. At noon, I went down to the Trzesniewski Buffet for a salmon and onion sandwich and a glass of beer, but as my quest took hold of me, I found it difficult to leave Freud's study, even for a coffee in the afternoon. I gazed at the orchids. I felt the tension in the room between candor and secrecy. I admired the Roman oil lamps, the carved jade and ivory, the little gods watching me, wondering if it was the beekeeper's acknowledgement of me that had produced my courage to travel to Vienna and boldly wait for Freud.

The dark leaves of the acacia drew the sunlight from the book-lined room, and all the time it was as though the beekeeper were standing just behind me. Could I ever walk up the stairs with him? Would he be the one to unbutton my dress and ease it down over my shoulders? I thought of the bees marking a stick or a leaf with a scent that invited the female to mate. I remembered our conversations. But could a woman who hasn't known love know what to feel, what to say, what to ask for, what to give back? This is what Freud had to tell me, and so one night, I stayed in the courtyard very late, long after the caretaker had locked up the rooms and gone home.

A single orange light burned in Freud's study, with moths fluttering around it. Bright strips of moonlight wavered over my arms, lit up my hair. I hesitated, then with an odd, ecstatic sensation, I climbed up the iron fire stairs behind the building, raised the old window on the second floor and stepped inside the room. Freud's statuettes stood in a row on his desk with a look of surprise in their eyes.

Everything smelled of rose oil, and the thick scent of hyacinths lulled me into a reverie. When I opened my eyes, I was lying on Freud's couch. He was sitting in his velvet chair beside the blue tile stove. So alive was the room with both the living and the dead that his presence did not seem surprising. His skin was gold and wrinkled. His black hair was neatly combed and parted on the left side. His beard was trimmed to a fine point. His dark brown eyes were luminous. "You've come with your misery," he said. "But the psychiatrist cures the neurotic misery in order to introduce the patient to the common misery of life."

"No," I said. "I'm in love. I've brought my happiness."

"We are never as defenseless against suffering as when we love," he said. "It's always the struggle between Eros and death. The evolution of civilization may even be described as the struggle of the human species for existence." Then he smiled and said, "Love may end in age and pain and mourning and regret—but love always begins in joy."

I did not know what to say. Hadn't I read that Freud found it difficult to keep professional confidences? I told him about Jasmine. "I think about the color of her eyes. I go to sleep smelling her perfume and wake up imagining she's cooking me oatmeal."

"Don't you ever dream of her?"

"Once I dreamed she shot me."

I told him about my hesitancies with the beekeeper and he said, "So you have the enjoyment of sticking your bare leg outside the bedclothes on a cold winter's night, then drawing it in again." He paused for a moment, his fingers smoothing down his beard. "The mob give vent to their impulses, and we deprive ourselves. We do so in order to maintain our integrity. We economize with our health, our capacity for enjoyment, our forces. We save up for something, not knowing ourselves for what.

And this habit of constant suppression gives us the character of refinement. We also feel more deeply and therefore dare not demand much of ourselves. Why do we not get drunk? Because the discomfort and shame of the hangover gives us more 'unpleasure' than the pleasure of getting drunk. Why don't we fall in love over again every month? Because with every parting, something of our heart is torn away. Why don't we make a friend of everyone? Because the loss of him or any misfortune happening to him would bitterly affect us. Thus our striving is more concerned with avoiding pain than with creating joy."

The little Buddha was watching me, and looking back at him, I saw how it could be between two people. The room was quiet except for the sound of water boiling in the reservoir of the stove. Freud was saying, "You are an artist—use your paint, your clay, your stone, your words, your sounds." But I was already passing the glass case filled with figurines, and by the time I opened the window, he had vanished into a haze of slow-moving smoke.

🜂 🜁

I ended up serving the beekeeper all Jasmine's favorite foods: lima beans, French fries, cole slaw, baked potatoes with cheese, cinnamon buns, Oreos. He sat at my small kitchen table, sweet in the light of the beeswax candles, wearing a plaid shirt, his green eyes watching me. I had dreamed of many men, but they were dark and they scared me, or else they were like Freud, shimmering with stature. But with the beekeeper in my house, I wanted to close the Venetian blinds, stop the clocks, sprinkle sunflower pollen over us, sit smiling at him hour after hour. The little house, heaped with hollyhocks and blue delphinium, softened around us with its pink flowered wallpaper, its crooked walls, its moss-covered roof. I sat across from him at the table. I was wearing a blue striped cotton dress with lace on the bodice and had pinned a marigold in my hair. We talked about the weather, the bees. I felt he had always been sitting there.

"The way to a man's heart is through his stomach, my mother says—so she said I should cook you a steak," I said. "But I couldn't cook anything that once dreamed and thought. Could you?"

"I always could eat a steak—till I got my bees. But then I started being with them, knowing them, and them knowing me. I never really thought about insects or any creature very much. But you spend hours and hours with these bees, watching over them, and it makes you think you owe them something."

I would tell him everything—about Jasmine, about Freud, about Father McCrory, about my birth. He would think I made up the life to amuse him, to please him, to weave stories for men as Jasmine did, to make him laugh. But he would not laugh. He would look at me as though he were gazing into the five eyes of a bee. A bee sits on her white eggs in the cell of the honeycomb, keeping the cold air away. Now I could hear it clearly—the rhythm of our bare feet tapping on the stairs, and in the morning a fragrant mist would rise up out of the hollyhocks growing around my tiny house.

The Finalists

❧ *Enoch Arden's One Night Stands* ❧

JACOB M. APPEL

THE PELICAN CITY YOUNG WIDOWS & WIDOWERS BEREAVEMENT
Circle met every Tuesday evening in the art/music/dance room of the
Pelican Harbor Jewish Day School. The room itself was cluttered with
the odd chaff of children's festivity: stacks of miniature xylophones, a
pink tutu abandoned on an old gymnastics mat, finger paintings suspended along a line like laundry. Alex—who had arrived nearly an hour
early—did not wish to be the first to cross the threshold. Instead he
waited outside in the under-lit corridor. Here the walls had been painted
a cloying institutional yellow. Glass cases ran along both sides of the
passageway, one documenting the history of the Holocaust through pho-
tography and the other relating local efforts to rehabilitate injured mana-
tees, the parallel displays reflecting the heaped carcasses of Mauthausen
and Ravensbrück onto newspaper images of beached aquatic fauna. Alex
paced the length of the manatee exhibit, skimming the articles from the
Harbor Gazette with nervous indifference, before suddenly latching onto
the dangers of aiding sea mammals: That's how Karen had died, he decided. It was as promising a lie as any.

Although he'd had twenty-six months to decide precisely what had
killed Karen, Alex had only given it meaningful thought in the five weeks
since Big Mitch suggested a support group. "It's not just about what it's
about, boss," the one-armed sous-chef had prodded him. "When I was
in NA, nobody went to get clean. Half the women there were there
for cock," he added. "And the other half were there for pussy." Maybe, thought Alex. But you couldn't show up for grief counseling if your
spouse was still alive, he knew, so he imagined ways to kill her off: *My
wife was devoured by alligators. My wife was kidnapped by pirates. My wife
was vaporized by pioneers from the Andromeda Galaxy.* He strove to keep
the scenarios as implausible as possible—to avoid all thought of serial
rapists and ocean undertows—and in the end he was back at square zero.
So why not death by sea cow? He'd say that Karen had detoured from
her afternoon jog to comfort a stranded manatee, and the creature had

dragged her off to Davey Jones' locker. He'd say....

Alex's eyes grew moist; he dared not wipe them. People passed behind him in the corridor—beneath the Israeli flag and into the room with the undersized chairs attached to undersized desks. Alex did not look up. His entire body rebelled against these first awkward moments of knowing nobody, enflaming his forehead, flushing the tips of his ears, so he did what he often did at weddings and parties: He focused all of his earthly attention on the first inanimate object to cross his gaze, which in this case happened to be the final glass panel in the manatee display. Staring back at him—all of her earthly attention focused on the Holocaust photographs to his rear—shone the petrified dark eyes of a young female reflection.

☙ ❧

Causes of death, it turned out, played little role in group bereavement. The widows and widowers did not gather in a conclave and introduce themselves like alcoholics: *My name is John, I'm thirty-five, my wife toppled off a Ferris wheel; I'm Mary, forty-two, my husband skimped on second-rate fugu.* While the facilitator, Charlotte Ann, spoke at some length about the three drunk teenagers who'd shattered her husband's canoe with their speedboat, the other survivors—Will, Natalie, T.J., Tina, G-Man, Sammy B. and Joanna—steered clear of the morbid. They told stories of ski trips and tailgate parties; they complained about delinquent babysitters and the awkward prospect of introducing a new girlfriend to old in-laws. Alex grew anxious for each speaker. He wanted them to go over well—for their sakes. When it came time for the delicate, dark-eyed girl named Joanna to unburden herself, he thought of her reflection and how he had looked away too suddenly, and now he positively trembled. It was her first meeting too. She told of how her husband had once been clawed by a cat at his office on the afternoon before a charity dinner-dance, and how that evening when she accompanied him into the unisex restroom at the Cormorant Arms hotel to change the dressings on his wounds, the door jammed shut behind them. "So I manage to tear my gown practically in half, working on the lock," said Joanna. "And I'm shouting. And I'm crying. Help me! Let me out! The whole nine yards. When the security guy finally gets the door open, there I am with the front of my dress ripped open and Owen sitting on the toilet seat with his shirt off and scratch marks all over his chest and neck." The girl spoke very quickly, in desperate bursts. She couldn't have been more than twenty-five. When she finished her story, Alex realized that he was smiling directly at her.

Charlotte Ann thanked Joanna. Others murmured assent. "Anyone else?" asked the facilitator.

Everyone except for Alex had spoken. He looked down at the top of his miniature desk. A choppy hand had scrawled on the wood: *Why couldn't Helen Keller drive? Because she was a woman. Why couldn't Helen Keller read? Because she was from Alabama.* She'll adjourn the meeting, Alex thought, and I'll never come back. Nearby, the equine woman named Natalie reached for the jacket on the back of her chair.

"*That* man," chirped Joanna. "He hasn't had a chance."

Alex suddenly found himself at stage center.

Charlotte Ann grinned. "Would *that man* like a chance?" she asked.

"Sure," lied Alex. "Why not?" And then he told the story of the night he'd proposed to Karen—when they were both only eighteen and living up north in Trenton, New Jersey. Her stepfather had owned a downtown bowling alley. Alex worked there as the manager on weekend evenings. During the pre-dawn darkness, the deserted Capital Lanes were an ideal setting for a lovers' tryst. Every Saturday night for nearly a year, Alex drove his future father-in-law home—and as soon as the old man entered the house, his daughter snuck out of the shrubbery for the return trip to the sofa in the bowlarama office. Until the March of their senior year. On the final day of that month, a Sunday, a mini-blizzard swept through Trenton after midnight. It's heavy, wet snow clung to the burgeoning leaves like webbing. When Alex and Karen arrived at the bowling alley for their rendezvous, a robust white oak had already plummeted through both the roof and the ceiling. Drifts rose waist-high on the lanes around the tree; frost seeped its way along the metal gutters like blood. The automatic pin setters had also gone haywire, toppling and replacing in a berserk game of chicken and egg. Alex was about to phone his employer when Karen's first snowball hit him smack between the eyes, and soon the two of them were on the slick floor of lane seven, groping and giggling, planning a wedding and a honeymoon in Florida. "I miss her," said Alex. "You know."

"Of course, honey," said Charlotte Ann. "We know."

Alex looked over at Joanna to see how his story had gone over, but she was diligently scribbling in a notebook. He tried to delay his own exit. He sat back down again and wrote on his desk: *Why couldn't Helen Keller find a husband?* Alex didn't know exactly why he was waiting, what he was waiting for. Soon he and the delicate girl were the only two people left in the room. When she shut her notebook, she appeared startled to find him still in his seat.

"Oh goodness," she said. "I'm so sorry. About before."

Alex thought back to the reflection in the glass.

"You didn't want to say anything, did you? I realized that as soon as I said something. I'm stupid that way—I was just writing about it in my journal."

"No big deal," said Alex. He didn't like the expression *stupid that way*; he suddenly felt disappointed, almost betrayed.

"What you said was so romantic, though. All that snow reminded me of *Ethan Frome*."

Alex walked her to the elevator and they rode down the three stories in silence. It was only nine o'clock and the summer dusk greeted them on the boardwalk outside. Silhouettes of wood storks crisscrossed the horizon. Alex searched for words to continue the conversation.

"It's a book," said Joanna. "You're wondering about *Ethan Frome*. It's a book, not a movie."

"Okay."

"I'm an English teacher," added Joanna.

"Okay."

Alex focused on two small green lizards darting along the wooden planks. Across the school parking lot, a pickup truck churned dust in its wake.

"I need to unwind after that," said Joanna. "Do you know a good place to eat?"

The lizards ducked under the railing. "You're in luck," said Alex, smiling, relaxing. "I own a restaurant."

"Is it good?"

JACOB M. APPEL — 25

Nobody had ever asked that before. It was like asking if he was good in bed.

"Not without Karen," he answered, mechanically. "Not any more."

🦅 🦅

Alex revealed his secret over a sizzling platter of Apalachicola oysters and mussels mariniere. They were ensconced at one of the corner booths in the Quarterdeck Room, swaddled by antique barometers and mollusk-draped rigging. The early bird crowd had long since departed, and through the swinging doors to the kitchen resounded the clash and clatter of the Captain's Mast readying for slumber. "A good restaurant needs beauty sleep, coddling," he said. "When we first bought this place from Karen's aunt and uncle, we tried to run it late into the night. We learned the hard way: The best bistros eat breakfast in bed." Alex refilled his wine glass, conscious of his tongue growing loose in his mouth. "I'm boring you to tears, aren't I?"

"No," answered the girl. "Not particularly."

Alex fumbled with his napkin ring. He regretted his vignette on the history of Oysters Rockefeller—but what else was he supposed to say? Seafood and Karen were the only two things he knew anything about.

A thin smile trailed across Joanna's lips, then faded. "That was supposed to be a joke," she said too quickly. "The *not particularly*."

Alex nodded. "My wife's not dead."

He braced for anger—Karen's temper would have flared. Joanna merely dabbed her lips with her napkin and waited for more.

"She's missing," he said. "Vanished off the face of the earth."

Joanna toyed with her wedding ring; he wondered if this meant something.

"One day she went out jogging" he continued, "and she jogged straight off into oblivion. They had search teams combing the beach for weeks, but nothing. Not so much as a tennis shoe." When Joanna said nothing—just focused on him with her intense, sooty eyes—he let himself go. He spoke of the days squandered leafleting shopping malls, the exertions whose eventual purpose grew merely to fend off suspicion. And he spoke of the uncertainty, the frustrations, the second-guessing.

How could he know whether she'd been carried away, gouging and claw-ing, or absconded fully of her own volition? How did he know if she'd show up again one day—at fifty? At eighty? He read in the paper about missing schoolgirls escaping from cults, amnesiacs stumbling upon long lost spouses, Japanese kidnapees returning from North Korea. All this hope made his bed feel colder, his plight more desperate and urgent. "Every time I accept that she might be dead, something reminds me that she's still alive….But when I get to thinking she's coming back, death throws me a zinger." Alex tore the top off a pack of artificial sweetener and poured the grains into his water glass, watching them form a sheet of frost on the surface. "Sometimes I dream of footprints on sand," he said. "Shallow footprints filling with murky water."

Joanna reached forward as though to take his hand, but she stopped, tentatively, several inches short. "How awful. Like Enoch Arden."

Alex nodded. "You mentioned that earlier."

"Did I?" puzzled the delicate girl. "Oh, no. That was *Ethan Frome*. This is Enoch Arden. It's a poem by Alfred Lord Tennyson."

"Next time around," said Alex, "I'll go to college."

"It's about this woman, Annie, whose husband is shipwrecked at sea," continued Joanna. "And presumed dead. Only he's actually not dead—and he comes back to find her married to a new man—"

"—named Enoch Arden—"

"—*named* Philip Ray. It's one of those popular misconceptions that the new husband is named Enoch Arden. The *old husband* was named Enoch Arden. Sort of like how some people think the one-armed man was The Fugitive."

Alex stirred the saccharine frosting in his water glass. "Okay," he agreed.

"But here's the important part," said Joanna—her face suddenly aglow like a schoolgirl with gossip. "Enoch doesn't reveal himself to An-nie. He loves her too much to ruin her happiness, so he conceals himself in a boarding house and dies alone."

The room turned silent. From the kitchen came the sound of Big Mitch hurling profanities at the industrial dishwasher. "So you're saying that Karen's out there somewhere. Hiding."

The delicate girl wilted. "I don't know what I'm saying," she said, unmoored. "You should read it."

"If I should, then I will." He reached across the table to fill his wine glass one last time. The thought crossed his mind that he had revealed too much and she too little. Good clams enter the pot closed and exit open. His instincts told him that the same rule applied to women and dinner. "And what about you? What's your story?"

"My story?" The delicate girl flicked back her long sable hair. "My story," she announced with sudden decision, "is that it's nearly eleven thirty and I'm teaching *Anna Karenina* tomorrow at eight."

"That's a book," said Alex, grinning. "Not a person."

She stood up and walked briskly toward the door.

"Next week," said Joanna.

Alex agreed—though he wasn't certain what he was agreeing to. "Next week."

❧ ❧

That night he missed Karen more than he had in months. Her absence actually afflicted him as physical pain, as a jab somewhere deep within his skull. Ever since losing his wife, Alex had abandoned their queen-size bed. He slept on the moth-gnawed olive sofa in the living room—to hear the door chime, in case she returned in the dark without keys. The couch itself was a stunted little pallet that Karen had once tagged a loveseat with ambitions. It didn't even let him stretch his legs. Yet now, for the first time, this constricted berth struck Alex as far too roomy, and he pitched about on the cushions for hours like a toy boat lost at sea. Shortly after three a.m., he retreated to the lanai. He sat at the end of a dew-soaked chaise longue. He wore only boxer shorts. The breeze off the ocean sent chills down his spine. In the pine barrens that rose beyond the bougainvillea hedge, scarlet ibises roosted like Christmas ornaments. So many of his nights with Karen had been spent in this little nook of paradise—reveling in the shock of their own successes. He could still hear her boasting, her voice slurred with sherry, "The *fucking* American dream!" That was the bare-knuckles Karen speaking, the hardscrabble New Jersey schoolgirl. She was the cart that drove the horse. Alex could not imagine loving anybody different.

When dawn broke, Alex went to market. Karen's uncle had taught him to inspect each fish individually at the wholesalers—to hand-pick the largest pompano, the tilapia and grouper still flailing in the stalls. The work required sharp eyes, stamina. Sometimes a thick apron. Not surprisingly, his arrival at the two-room municipal library several hours later—his work boots and dungarees still lacquered in snook guts—drew the attention of the puffy, chinless young man behind the counter. The youth folded his stubby arms across his breast. "Need any help?"

"Just looking," muttered Alex. Libraries and bookstores generally made him feel self-conscious, and this attendant's polite offer stung like an accusation of shop-lifting. The problem was he'd forgotten the poet's name. He had no choice. He walked briskly to the main desk. "Do you have Enoch Arden?"

The librarian looked up from a crossword puzzle. "Is that a book or an author?"

"It's a poem," retorted Alex. "I don't know who wrote it."

He waited for the librarian to snicker, but the young man merely smiled in sympathy. "That's hard, if you don't know the poet's name."

"It's a famous poem," said Alex.

The librarian scratched the pink flesh around his collar. "You know what I'll do," he said. "I'll phone my grandmother." The youth flicked open his cellular phone, adding in a more professional voice: "She reads a lot."

They finally found *Tennyson—Selected Poems* in the children's room; it had been propped against one of the windows to keep the air-conditioner from blowing open the drapes.

※ ※

The delicate woman didn't show up the following week, or the next. Alex had arrived early both evenings in the hope of discussing Enoch and Philip and Annie Lee. He'd also tackled "In Memoriam" and "The Charge of the Light Brigade"—the idea of knowing something other than shellfish *did* appeal to him—but it was Arden's turmoil that he burned to explore. She'd said next week, hadn't she? A promise, a contract. What sort of person plays so fast and loose with her words? Alex understood that he had no legitimate gripe against the woman—she'd made an idle remark to a virtual stranger, nothing more—but he didn't care. So what if his anger was irrational? Anger *wasn't* rational. On the occasion of Joanna's second absence, Alex shared the Enoch Arden tale with the rest of the support group. Philip Ray, the second husband, sent Sammy B. into a dither. His own dead wife, it turned out, had been unfaithful. G-Man called Enoch a "chicken-shit bastard" who deserved what he got. When Tina stood up for the hapless fisherman—"it's just like on *The Days of Our Lives*," she insisted—the two went at each other's throats. Eventually, they both turned on Alex. He apologized: "It was stupid to bring up." For the remainder of the meeting, he kept silent. His attention drifted, and he counted the colored tags that labeled the walls, the windows, the chalkboard in both Hebrew and transliterated English. He read the wisdom on his desktop: *Abe Lincoln was Jewish. He was shot in the temple.* Also: *Lucy eats snotburgers, Chazz & Lindsay 4ever.* In response to *Why couldn't Helen Keller find a husband?* someone had inked *Because she was a lesbian.* Alex snuck a glance at his watch. At the Captain's Mast, Big Mitch would be rolling out the first of the key lime pie.

I'm not coming back, he decided. Enough is enough.

He did, of course. He arrived early again—planning to ask the facilitator if she knew the delicate woman's last name, seething with two week's pent up frustrations—to discover Joanna standing in the corridor and sipping coffee from a Styrofoam cup. She wore a low-cut cotton dress. The fine ridges of her collarbone danced with every breath. Alex examined her reflection in the glass display case—where a tribute to Israeli astronaut Ilan Ramon had replaced the manatee exhibit. Everything about her struck him as so fragile, almost ethereal: her slender shoulders, her perfect teeth aligned like small white tombstones. A contrast to his wife's substance, fullness—to Karen's fleshy thighs and the breasts he could palm like baby pumpkins. In the glass, he traced Joanna's fine features—superimposed upon a profile of the space shuttle at dawn, reflecting also the death chamber atrocities and swastika-emblazoned banners from the opposing glass case—to uncover his own reflection, and her eyes once again locked upon his. He shifted his gaze to the fringes of the Shuttle Columbia portrait and examined them with a sudden and ferocious intensity. She reeled to face him, leaving his eyes no escape.

"You're back," she said. "I'm so glad."

His anger—what was left of it—turned upon him. All of his past frustrations now seemed so unreasonable, so utterly overblown. "I read the poem," he said.

The threads of her eyebrows rose in uncertainty.

"Enoch Arden," said Alex. "I wanted to tell you how much I enjoyed it, but you weren't here...."

"Oh, Tennyson," answered Joanna. "I'm so glad you liked it. Many people don't, you know."

Alex tucked his thumbs into the pockets of his slacks. It hadn't crossed his mind that G-Man and Sammy B. were in the majority—that *he* was the odd man out. "I don't know much about poems," he said. "All I know is what I like."

Joanna nodded. "Some people find Arden a bit too...forced, maybe hackneyed. All that Victorian gloom and doom. I like to think Enoch must have had a mistress tucked away somewhere, maybe more than one...." The woman paused, bit her lip. She added disdainfully: "Tennyson would never tell us that, of course."

"Of course," echoed Alex.

He followed her into the meeting room. His entire understanding of the poem had suddenly come loose at the hinges—and all the questions he'd had for the delicate woman no longer seemed relevant. After Karen's disappearance, Alex had seriously wondered whether she might have been having an affair. How could he not? Yet if that were the case—and deep down he didn't accept it—then he'd always assumed the transgression and her absence to be linked. Either she'd run off with this unknown man, or he'd done to her the unspeakable. A third possibility now confronted him: Maybe his wife had been unfaithful *independent* of her disappearance. Everybody had secrets, after all. One look around the circle at his grief-stricken companions—all of whom except Joanna and Charlotte Ann had already confessed to cheating—reminded him how easy it must be to become enmeshed in the tangled gossamer of infidelity.

Joanna told the circle about her trip with Owen to the Galapagos—of how they'd watched the mating dances of the blue-footed boobies and how her husband had tried to replicate them in their cabin. Alex didn't reveal anything. He waited for her at the end of the meeting, but the equine woman named Natalie had visited the ladies' room, and now shared their elevator ride. Natalie also had a connection to the Galapagos, having watched a Discover Channel special. She peppered Joanna with inanities about giant tortoises and tropical penguins. Mercifully, the woman's ride awaited her at the curbside. Without warning, Alex and Joanna stood alone. The insect lamp drove their long shadows toward the cusp of oblivion.

"You weren't here last week," said Alex.

Joanna held her hands clasped in front of her.

"I had a good time at dinner," she said. "I wasn't ready for that."

Alex rustled in his pocket for his keys. "The mussels were tender, weren't they?"

Joanna smiled. "Passable," she said.

She nodded in the direction of the beach—and they walked down the boardwalk, alongside the cast-iron benches and topiary shrubs. Beyond the grassy dunes, the distant surf murmured through the darkness. "Do you want to know?" she asked.

"I wouldn't have asked."

"Owen drove off the Cormorant Island causeway," she said.

"Intentionally?"

Joanna shrugged her frail shoulders. "Who knows? He was a pediatric dentist…. One of the girls said things….said he did things….."

"Oh Jesus," said Alex. "Was it….?"

"How the hell should I know?" slashed Joanna. "She was goddam *thirteen*."

She paused and drew in her breath; she made no effort to dampen her tears. "I'm sorry. You didn't deserve that." The young woman stretched her arms, opening her hands as though to cast away anger like feed grain. "Uncertainty," she said.

"You're telling me," answered Alex. "Dinner?"

Her nod was faint, fleeting—yet it was a nod. And over dinner they discussed lighter topics: the rare yellow lobster on display at the Tampa aquarium, the ongoing boycott of sea bass and bluefin tuna. Joanna had her own take on shellfish: She related how Cleopatra had dissolved a pearl earring in wine to prove Egypt's wealth to Marc Antony, how

Chekhov had written of oysters, and later how the playwright's coffin had been transported from Germany to Moscow on a freight car labeled "For Oysters Only." She also spoke of her interest in poetry. She'd arrived at literature "late in life"—she'd actually studied marine biology in college, but had killed time reading while waiting for "scientific magic" in the lab—and, at the end of the evening, she even recited Browning's "My Last Duchess" to the delight of the kitchen staff.

"Encore," demanded the one-armed sous-chef. "Encore"

"Next week," she promised—to Alex, to Big Mitch, to the twin busgirls Susana and Mariana. "You've worn me out."

She stopped Alex from walking her to her car: "Next week."

When he returned to the kitchen—half jubilant, half on-edge—Big Mitch cut the ground out from under him. "She isn't nothing like Karen," he said. "Not better or worse, you know. Just a different cut of meat."

🍂 🍃

"How do you break up with someone you're not dating?" Alex asked Big Mitch.

They were standing on either side of the seafood station, shucking oysters. Alex had already jabbed himself twice. A few stray shells lay in a puddle of bloody water on the countertop. Alex admired Big Mitch's dexterity. The sous-chef held each oyster in his one large hand—and carved it with a thick makeshift blade strapped to his thumb.

"Fucking depends," said Big Mitch. "You breaking up with her to start dating her? Or you breaking up to get rid of her?"

Alex stuck his knife into the wooden cutting board. He dabbed horseradish on a raw oyster and sucked the tiny body into his mouth. "Good flavor in these Olympias," he said. "Try one."

"Not in May," said the sous-chef. The conventional wisdom—long since trumped by commercial farming—warned against oysters in months whose names did not contain the letter "r". The sous-chef carried his cache of mollusks to the shellfish refrigerator. "Nothing romantic about getting the runs."

"I don't know what I want," said Alex. "She didn't show up again last week. That's four meetings out of the last seven."

The sous-chef returned and carried off Alex's store of oysters. "Why the fuck don't you just ask her out? Take her dancing or something?"

"Jesus Christ," said Alex. "I'm married."

The sous-chef shrugged his one good shoulder. "Don't stop most people," he said. "And if you're so married, boss, where's your wife at?"

The ceiling fan buzzed overhead like a helicopter. Big Mitch stepped into the alcove bathroom and left the door open; Alex heard his urine hitting the water. "You're way out of line," shouted Alex.

The toilet flushed; the faucet ran. "So fucking fire me," called the sous-chef. He returned with the fronds of his hawaiian shirt poking though his fly.

They glared at each other: Alex's eyes flashed sharp and hot against Big Mitch's unflappable durability. The sous-chef's exposed stump—a birth defect, not a war injury—suggested courage, street smarts. Eventually, Alex looked away. His gaze settled on a shiny silver pot brimming with crushed ice.

"It's me I should fire," he said. "How about bowling?"

❧ ❧

The enterprise proved far easier than Alex had anticipated. He offered; she accepted. That evening—after a raucous meeting in which Sammy B. publicly declared his love for an unsuspecting Tina—they braved a torrential Gulf Coast squall, which had flooded shut the interstate, and followed the mangrove-lined back roads to Sawgrass Bowling & Billiards. Joanna drove: a beige Dodge Dart from the late 1970's that resembled a giant cigar on roller skates. The car's interior smelled of spearmint, of lemongrass, of woman's shampoo. Hand-knit hoods covered the seat backs; baby pink Mardi Gras beads dangled from the overhead light. Magazine clippings—cartoons, photographs—were scotch taped to the face of the dashboard. Alex's father, a transmission specialist from Camden, always insisted that cars mirrored souls. That theory made Joanna spiritual, complicated. Alex's own pickup stank pungently of ocean musk—evaporated brine, mackerel viscera—which also struck him as an unfortunate confirmation of his father's hypothesis.

"When was the last time you went bowling?" asked Alex.

"You'll laugh," answered Joanna. "I've never been."

"Never?"

Joanna squinted through the sheets of rain. "Owen had a bad knee. He fell off a horse as a kid." Something inchoate and feral cut across the road; Alex's foot reached for an imaginary brake. "It's amazing, you know, how people define each other. *Owen* had a bad knee, so *I* never went bowling."

"With Karen it was airplanes," said Alex. "Scared the living shit out of her."

His own use of the past tense caught him off guard.

"I love flying," said Joanna. "It's like magic."

The glowing, low-slung form of the Sawgrass Lanes rose suddenly against the gray horizon. A sign out front flashed "OWL" "OWL" "OWL" in neon—the burned out "B" hunkered down against the storm. If Karen's father was running the place, thought Alex, he'd have me out there changing bulbs in a hurricane. But the old man was dead, of course. Diabetes. Renal failure. Too independent, too stubborn, for dialysis. Yet the interior of the Sawgrass Lanes—that septic junior high school stench, poorly lacquered over with cleanser and verbena—pricked at Alex's memory. A list of 300 game bowlers ran the height of one wall; a case of league trophies traversed the length of another. In the far corner, near a decapitated payphone, teenagers clustered around an arcade game. Somewhere out of view, Alex sensed, hid an manager's office with a sofa.

"What do we do first?" asked Joanna. "You've got to tell me what to do, you know. I don't want to mess up."

Alex steered them to the shoe-exchange counter. Thunder from outside melded with the crash of falling pins. "There's only one important rule in bowling," he said. "You want to make sure you keep the ball on your own lane."

"Like driving," said Joanna.

"You've got it," said Alex. "I've never thought of that."

Joanna examined her bowling shoes suspiciously; they were the smallest size. "You'll teach me step by step?" she asked.

"I promise. Just like swimming."

They were already through nine frames—with Alex leading 186 to 47—when the conversation rapidly veered away from bowling. It was all Alex's doing, though he wasn't sure what prompted him. Maybe the 50's music, maybe the college kids on a double date in the adjacent lane. "Those poets," he said, apropos of nothing. "Browning. Tennyson. Swinburne. They must have gotten lonely."

Joanna sat down beside him on the plastic aqua bench. She held her bowling ball between her legs, as though she'd just given birth to a boulder. "Swinburne?"

Alex had discovered Swinburne on his own; he now feared that he'd pronounced the poet's name incorrectly. "What I mean is—it must get lonely doing all that writing."

"I always think it's worse for the characters," answered Joanna. "They're stuck forever in the same bad relationships. Poor Hester, poor Anna. But sometimes I think it's all a pack of lies—that Emma Bovary was actually messing around with Homais the chemist."

"Yes," agreed Alex. "'Or that Enoch Arden was having one night stands."

Immediately they both realized that they were no longer talking about what they were talking about. Joanna fumbled with the gold bangles around her wrists; sometime since their first meeting, Alex realized, she'd removed her wedding band. He glanced nervously around the alley. Most of the other lanes stood empty. One of the college couples had departed early, while the other had given up bowling. The girl now sat on the guy's lap—and he clearly had his hand under her skirt. Women inside, Alex remembered, feel like squid.

"There's a scene in *Anna Karenina*," said the delicate woman in a wispy voice, "in which this learned intellectual named Sergey Ivanovitch and a poor relation named Varenka go out mushroom picking...."

Alex's lower back had started to cramp—too much bending—but he dared not stretch. From the seat behind them came the desperate sounds of giggling or whimpering; he focused hard on Joanna.

"...They have this moment," she continued. "Out in the forest. Where either he'll propose—where something will happen between them, or it will all be over forever...."

Joanna looked up; a thin smile traced her trembling lips.

Alex felt his own body fluttering. He knew something was called for—statement, action. A charge of urgency swept through him, priming his senses, magnifying the odor of floor polish and the clatter of pins. But with his heightened emotions came the sudden tug of the past—flashing before him that lost moment of youthful enrapture on lane seven, the groping, the fumbling, Karen's long auburn hair dappled with frost. He could feel her snow-numb nose meeting his—like Eskimos. The memory reached for him like a hand reaching forth from the grave. Alex found his focus entirely derailed and he stared blankly at Joanna. Her eyes remained wide and hopeful. She was waiting for him to speak.

"*Anna Karenina*," Alex said finally. "I've never read it." He struggled for something further and added: "Is it good?"

Joanna opened her mouth to answer, but didn't. Across the alley came a ripple of plangent euphoria—someone had toppled his tenth straight strike. Alex watched the fellow high-fiving his buddies.

"Yes, of course," said Joanna sharply. "It's good."

She stood up and walked rapidly to the ladies' room. After that, they bowled out the last frame, speaking only when necessary, and she drove him home.

🦅 🦅

The storm worsened past midnight. The wind picked up something fierce, slashing palm branches against the siding of the bungalow. Alex sat on the edge of the threadbare couch in his boxer shorts. He wanted something to happen—he wanted the doorbell to ring. "Ring the goddam bell," he thought. "Just ring the goddam bell!" Whether he was speaking to his missing wife, or to the delicate woman, even he no longer knew. Around three a.m.—shortly after the power went dead—he lit a candle and read to himself the opening passages of *Enoch Arden*. He grew drowsy. The words waltzed aimlessly under the lambent flame. Alex kept waiting, irrationally, for Enoch to reveal himself to his wife. He didn't of course. When the tears came to Alex's eyes, he folded shut the book and retreated to the master bedroom. He slammed shut the door behind him and slept with the thick down comforter pulled snug over his head. It was the deep, stony sleep of a man who'd died twice in one night.

❦ *The Wheelwright* ❦

STEPHENIE BROWN

JACOB WORKED SILENTLY. NO ONE WATCHED HIM, OR LISTENED to his commentary, or observed or tested the thoroughness of his work. But still he made himself do the job right. God was watching. You could feel God's eyes on you from the hot sky, the thick prairie grasses moving even when there was no wind.

Jacob licked his thumb and ran it around the perfect curving wood. He picked the wheel up, turning its edge to his chest and gripping a spoke in each hand. He slid his eyes around the rim, measuring the wheel's dish by sight, determining whether it had proper support for climbing a hill. Jacob's skilled arms shifted the wheel side to side and held it high, weighing and balancing it. It was a heavy wheel, but in Jacob's control it looked light.

"This town's lucky to have a man like you!" Franklin used to say when he watched Jacob tossing and tightening a wheel as if it were a spool of thread. In the afternoon, after closing his shop, Franklin had liked to stand at the rail and watch Jacob work. He'd smooth his hands down the rim of a wheel. "Don't know how you make 'em so solid. Strong. Real integrity in those wheels. We're sure lucky."

But Jacob lay awake at night wondering how his wheels would stand up if they were really and truly tested, if someone depended on them for survival. He twisted in his blanket and considered the Greeleys, man and wife, grandmother, two aunts too young to marry, a boy and girl and a baby. One wheel popped a spoke, then the extra wheel splintered. They were caught in a late spring blizzard at Round Blade. The father and the boy, Adam Greeley, who was fourteen years old, tried to track back for help. The boy made it out, and the rest froze to death, then thawed real sudden with the blooming wildflowers, the two young aunts huddled together and still pretty enough to kiss.

What would have happened if the Greeleys had used Jacob's wheels instead? Jacob's wheels might have saved them. They might have been able to drive through the storm. Or might not, but he still made every wheel perfect as he could.

Thinking of Adam Greeley, Jacob startled when he turned and saw a dusty boy leaning over the rail, watching him work.

"Whatcha doing?"

"Fitting the falloe, here, this bit, against the edge."

The boy watched. He kicked some dust with his toe.

"How old are you, son?"

"Thirteen."

"You from around here?"

"No. We're from Idaho Falls. Vacation."

"You in school?"

"Yeah."

"Like it?"

"It's alright."

Jacob worked and the boy watched. Jacob tightened, strengthened, fortified the wheel. The boy unwrapped a piece of chewing gum. Artificial watermelon fragrance wafted toward Jacob.

"Do you sell those things?"

Jacob's mouth hardened. He put down the wheel.

"We use them. Here."

"You could sell them. Online or something. Ever thought of that?"

Jacob turned to this thoughtful entrepreneur. The boy was polite. He was interested. There was no need to bite his head off.

"I don't think I could sell them, son."

"Sure you could. You could sell them to those actors. You know those people who do the civil war battles and stuff. Like who have all those big cannons and stuff they pull around." The boy spread his arms out, widened his eyes: *big cannons.*

At least the boy was interested. Better than the little video-brained techno-brat seventh graders at Sherman Middle School, which Jacob had been glad to see the last of, even if now he lived in a trailer.

"Those re-enactors use rubber and steel plates on their wheels. I don't do that."

"Bet it makes them last longer."

"It isn't authentic."

The boy nodded. He understood. It made sense to him, God bless him. But wait until college, wait until he went to work in a cubicle. Then he'd join the lot of them, thinking the best measure of a man is how fast he can move his soft fingers on a keyboard or sweet-talk a customer.

"You okay?"

"Yeah." Jacob sat down on a barrel that he had made himself. "Where's your folks?"

"Gift shop."

"You don't want anything?"

The boy shrugged.

Jacob looked around him, and his eyes settled on a particular object. He held it out. "Here."

"What is it?"

"Chisel. We made it here at the Township. We have to order the metal but I got the wood. Kyle 'round the corner does the metalwork."

The boy studied the even, balanced tool and its sweat-darkened handle. "Don't you need it?"

Jacob did need it, but suddenly didn't want it.

"Go on. You ought to have something authentic."

"Thanks." The boy looked embarrassed. He looked as if he wanted to leave, and then he did.

Jacob closed his station at four thirty, and stopped at the Carriage Inn to tell Kate he couldn't see her tonight.

She tugged at her modest skirt, and wiggled a little under it.

"Something wrong?"

"I've just got some things to do. In town."

She rubbed his arm, which she loved to do. She once suggested that he try to get a job modeling for romance novels, like Fabio. Of course Jacob didn't know who Fabio was. Kate had to explain. Then Jacob started to understand that Kate was really in it for the sexual thrill, not the historical one. She'd worked at Prairie Township three summers in a row, probably because Disney World didn't have any openings, but came back permanently for Jacob. She thought she had fallen in love with the prairie, with history, with Jacob's taciturn philosophy, but really she just liked rolling around with a strong man who didn't watch ESPN.

She tried to travel a bit with him. Sometimes they'd stay up at one of the rooms at the Inn. She'd fix a dinner on the wood stove, and they'd burn candles and light a fire, and she'd talk about life at the Township without any reference to how underpaid they all were.

Four or five of them traveled. Franklin, especially, traveled with panache. He could go days without mentioning any object or event after 1870. He tried to get them all to go to the plank-clad church Sundays and listen to him preach after the style of the Second Great Awakening. Franklin, Kyle, Mrs. Morris and Jacob used to gather Saturday evenings for Township meetings. Mrs. Morris never cheated in her cooking, never reached for the Crisco, and Jacob was always hungry and ate with perfect authenticity. They listened to Jacob's wisdom as he expounded on the troubles of the day, the Indians, the Grant administration. But the group indulged these practices furtively, like Trekkers who have joined a law firm but keep whispering Klingon to one another in the bathrooms. Other Township employees would scoff if they knew the seriousness of their desires, the deprivations they suffered voluntarily. The others would snicker, and ruin it all.

Then Franklin just quit. His heart had really been with the Civil War, sometimes even the Revolutionary War. He never quite found contentment on the Prairie, not even in those flashes of transcendent travel, those moments when he was Almost There. Mrs. Morris and Jacob figured he had gone off to join a troupe of re-enactors. Nearly a year after leaving, Franklin sent Jacob a letter, on parchment, written with a quill. He announced that he was joining the staff of a historical magazine, one which Jacob particularly scorned, and also that he was getting married. He concluded his missive thusly:

A Return to Reason

My Civil War Phase has ended for good
No longer do I care to know
The rankings and rows of the West Point classes
The training and triumphs from Mexico.

The generals blend now into One.
Wasn't it Wheeler, or Sheridan,

Who did that thing at that place somewhere
And altered the course of America?

Alternative histories escape me too,
If the British had broken the naval blockade…
If the smooth bore had hit not quite so true…
If the choice were made to retrench, not invade…

I argue neither pro nor con.
It's worn me out, I dare not try.

I've nothing left to give that war.
Its sagas leave my eyes quite dry.

I've stood at Traveler's grave and mourned
The death of my beautiful lunacy.

One could not argue with that. Jacob cringed, he twitched in a paroxysm of concentrated depression, and he missed work for a week. It would be hard to face life at Prairie Township without Franklin, whose force of personality was enough to make anyone join, gaily and eagerly, into a bit of re-enacting, even a bit of travel. Franklin had valued Jacob and Kyle and Mrs. Morris, and protected them from criticism. The Township could split apart so easily. The gift shop and leatherworkers, with their nifty inauthentic saddlebags, outnumbered and out-profited the authentic settlers who denied themselves even the pleasure of a soda pop in the air conditioning.

So Jacob was grateful for Kate's efforts now, even though he could see she mistook her motivation. Kate, bless her heart, bless her whole buxom body, was trying very hard. When they lay together in the Inn, he was sometimes Almost There, and sometimes, he believed he was There. Only the tiny flesh-colored patch on her hip, the thing that thankfully kept her from getting pregnant, reminded him that a world existed in which he was not indispensable, in which he was not building a community, in which he could not, like Lincoln, eventually become president.

How long would Kate remain self-deceived? If they were married, and had a child, would she want to keep living like this? She'd want him to teach school, and get one of those new houses that was brick on one side and vinyl on three, and give up making wheels.

But now her eyes were all disappointment and desire. She would promise him anything. Jacob kissed her on the forehead and apologized for missing their evening. He walked to the bus stop. He was going to see Charlotte again.

Jacob had seen Charlotte three times in the past ten years, but they still talked on the telephone nearly every week, and sometimes he wrote her letters. She called him her "best, most authentic, friend." Back in college he used to call her the "prettiest girl on the prairie," and she used to giggle and bat her long spidery eyelashes at him from under her blue calico bonnet, which was not exactly period authentic but was good enough. Sometimes her giggle grew into an uncontrolled chortle. He had wondered if, after her newness wore off, after they'd begun to spend a lifetime together, her laugh might begin to annoy him. But that worry had been needless for years. Now Charlotte had a rich fiancé. Someone she'd been dating six months but failed to mention. Bradley or Brady or something else coastal-sounding. He couldn't hear her properly on the answering machine. She'd started giggling, then chortling. Probably Bradley Brady was grabbing her from behind. Then the machine cut off, thank God.

Jacob walked past Prairie Hardware, Prairie Pancakes, Prairie Tacos, and the always busy Cheeseburger in Purgatory, owned by a Midwestern wit. He veered into the Prairie Diner, and saw Charlotte before she saw him.

And he also saw, for the first time, that Charlotte looked just like Kate. Why, maybe Charlotte *was* Kate, but older, smarter, and with an annoying laugh. He shook his head, he couldn't believe he'd never noticed it before. Charlotte had her arm around a pudgy little twerp. The twerp had an oily smile and an expensive-looking jacket which his belly hung out of, and his arm was slung nonchalantly, yet possessively, around Charlotte's shoulder. He had to reach up a little, because he was a short stout little ugly twerp.

"Jacob!" She wasn't going to hug him. But she reached out, touched his arm. "This is Brody."

"Brody." Jacob extended his hand, and Brody met him with an equally wrenching hand shake.

They sat in a booth and Brody ordered a Prairie Burger. Charlotte ordered a tuna salad, and Jacob ordered pork chops.

"It's good to see you, Charlotte."

"You look great."

"Thanks." *Was it possible that Charlotte had brought her new man all the way out here just to show him off? Why were they here?* Jacob looked at the door. He could leave.

Brody smirked. "It looks like this sort of life agrees with you."

"It does. I can't complain."

"No."

"Brody, did I mention Jake's written lots of papers on nineteenth century life? One was published just last month in, in…ah…"

"*The Utah Historical Review.* Yeah. But I'm not writing much any more. So how've you been, Charlotte?"

"Busy. But I'm still glad I started my company."

"You weren't the type who works for someone else."

"Look." Charlotte dug in her bag, and pulled out a card.

Jacob held it like a butterfly, flat in one rough open hand: "Charlotte Smith Décor. Discovering Your Authentic Self Through Interior Design!"

"That's how we met." Brody reached up and put an arm around Charlotte.

"Brody's a developer."

A developer. One who develops things. One who makes lots of money. Smart Charlotte.

"You'd like the things Brody develops. He doesn't build those awful McMansions. Not that kind of thing."

Dinner arrived. The waitress smiled at them all, but gave a special flirty, evaluating look to Jacob, whose shirt was a little open, and whose hair was a little shaggy, and whose muscles showed how hard he worked.

Not this way, darling. Look that way. The money's over on that side of the table. That's how evolution works these days. You'll see when you grow up.

"Charlotte's told me how real you are, Jake."

Real? "Real what?"

"Real nineteenth century, I guess she means. She said you don't even use a modern razor."

What's the point of this? "I'm doing what I want to do, instead of what popular culture dictates."

Brody smirked at Charlotte, as if to say, See?

Then he sniffed. "I guess deodorant isn't authentic either."

"No it isn't, and I was thinking of asking Charlotte to sit over here so I can sit next to you and hear all your smart comments better."

"Hey! Just kidding, man. We're all friends, right?" Brody looked around, as if the rest of the empty diner could bear witness to his good will.

Charlotte looked as if she were about to vomit and run away.

"I was trying to tell you, Jake, that you'd like the work Brody does." Charlotte's voice was throaty and shrill, a swallowed parakeet of a voice.

What does it matter whether I'd like it? Does she want me to approve and bless the union or something? Am I walking her down the aisle? "Well, good, I guess. I'm glad you think I'd like what Brody does."

Brody rubbed his chin. "Tell me about this article, Jake. The Utah thing."

"You could read it." *As if you ever read anything but the financial pages.*

"Sure. Do you have a copy on you?"

"No."

Brody shrugged amicably. "So why not tell me about it?"

"I wrote an article re-creating a trip West made by a family called the Greeleys."

"Did it take a lot of research?"

"Original papers were bequeathed to the Township. Adam Greeley wrote a lot. He's the one who survived the trip."

"Interesting. No, really. I really do think it's interesting. And you know, there's a place in the world for people who do research, who understand historical accuracy."

Charlotte leaned forward. "Jake, Brody develops historically-sensitive shopping centers."

"Lifestyle Centres."

"Lifestyle Centres. He's done them all over New England. They're fabulous. They have real accurate detail. You know, there are practical demands of course. But they're completely charming. It's really the latest thing, to have these centers, that are like what used to be the village green, where people can meet up, and listen to music, have a drink or coffee, and it's all pedestrian. They can shop, or not. It's so civilized. Some are large, for a whole community, and some are really small and cute. There's even an Italian one in a residential area in Northern Virginia. Where was that place, Brody?"

"Fox Glen Pointe at Crofte Hill Acres."

Good God.

Charlotte shrugged up her shoulders in apparent delight. "It's so quaint, with this gorgeous fountain, sort of like an Italian piazza."

"Because the Italians were great settlers of Virginia."

Brody took over. "That's not the point, Jake. History is moving forward." Brody paused, as if waiting for someone to write down what he said. "We, my company, are creating positive, livable space for people that comports with real human needs for society and community and physical activity."

Then why don't you get some?

"My company's work isn't so alienating, so blatantly consumerist, as those drive-up strip malls. I mean, you have to drive up and park *outside* our Lifestyle Centres and walk in, and sometimes it's quite a walk, I can tell you. And we try to fit them in to the lifestyle of the area, its history, its culture."

"Ah."

"And that's where you come in." Brody cast his eyes over to Charlotte, who smiled encouragement. "We're moving out West now. I got a contract outside Indianapolis to do a Lifestyle Centre. In fact, I expect we're gonna do about eight of them in the next four years in the Midwest."

"Congratulations." Jake said this to Charlotte.

"Thanks. But the thing is, I could use your help." Brody leaned in, all humble and earnest. "I need an expert on prairie lifestyles."

You must be kidding. "You must be kidding."

"No. Charlotte tells me you're the man for the job."

"Then Charlotte also told you I'd never do it."

"Well she did tell me I'd have to beg a little, but it would be worth it."

This guy would say anything.

"And the pay's not bad. Not bad. Look, Jake. Charlotte's told me how important history is to you. How living this *life* affects you. And believe it or not, I understand. Once I even did something sort of like what you're doing now. Would you believe, when I was twenty years old I quit college and went down to Bolivia?" Brody chuckled. "Bought myself a bar and ran it for two years. Got set up with a fine blond belly dancer and an alcoholic red howler monkey to keep me company. Do you believe me?"

"Sure." *I just don't care.*

"Now it was intense, and stimulating and life-altering and all that. And it was fine to make like Hemmingway or whatever for a little while. But it wasn't real. Not real. Do you know what I mean?"

Charlotte nodded. Jacob looked at the door again. Brody continued: "My man, you need to find out who you are right now, not 1860 whatever, and see about making yourself happy. And yeah, it wouldn't hurt to make some money. Everyone here knows you can do it. Charlotte goes on and on about how smart you are, how talented." Brody grinned and rubbed Charlotte's shoulder. "I was starting to get jealous."

Charlotte shoved Brody and giggled, looking down.

Great, I'm a little joke.

"I'm trying to help you out here, Jack. If Charlotte says you're the best man for the job, then you are. And if she says hiring you would be the smartest move I ever made, then I'm gonna do it. If you have all these talents, and I think you do, then you ought to turn them to some use. Man, you can't dedicate your entire life to building obsolete wheels."

Jacob stabbed his pork chop.

Charlotte reached a hand across the table, then drew it back. "It wouldn't be so bad, Jake. You could still do prairie things on the weekends. You could make wheels."

"She's right. You know, lots of people do history on the weekends. I mean, there's this whole other world out there, people who go out on Saturday and reenact Gettysburg or Lexington and Concord or the Battle of the Bulge. I...well maybe you need tanks for that one. But the point is, there are lots of normal people with normal jobs, making money, and come the weekends, they act out, being knights or ladies-in-waiting or pirates. You could do that, too." Brody winked. "Arrrgh! Ahoy, me hearties!"

Up yours with your own parrot, matey. "Would you kindly pass the butter?"

"It's margarine."

"Of course it's margarine. I'll still eat it."

Jacob margarined his roll with his butter knife. The roll was hot and yeasty, baked with enriched processed white flour. The margarine sank into the air pocket holes, and when Jacob dug the knife in deeper, a satisfying stream of steam arose.

"He's not even listening to me."

Charlotte reached over and grabbed Jacob's wrist. "Listen. Just listen, okay?"

"Why?"

"Why? Why?! Jacob, it's…Mabel worries about you. She asks about you, and what can I say?"

"How is Mabel?"

"Beautiful. She's not really a little girl any more."

"Is she going to call this guy 'Daddy'?"

Charlotte let go Jacob's wrist and pushed back into the booth. She folded her arms. Now her voice was like a hammer pinging an anvil: "You've seen her twice in her whole life. Twice. Her. Whole. Life."

"Three times."

"The day she was born doesn't count."

"Hey, hey, hey! Guys! We're cool? We're still all friends? Charlotte's explained it all to me, Jake. Mabel calls me 'Brody.' That's how we like it. This is a good thing for Mabel, Jake. A very good thing."

She'll have everything money can buy. "I wanted to see her more. I just don't like to fly. They moved."

"That's okay. That's cool. But you're going to have to get used to a little flying when you come work for me."

"I'm not going to come work for you."

"Charlotte wants you to. So do I."

Silence.

"So does Mabel. She's your girl, not mine. And I owe her this chance to see you more often. It's the least I can do for my Charlotte."

Jacob threw down his napkin and fork and knife and stood up, jarring the whole table, spilling two water glasses sideways and crashing a salad plate to the floor.

"Sit down. You're even worse than she said."

Charlotte put her face in her hands, and shook her head, and leaned away, distancing herself from them both. She wouldn't look up.

Jacob didn't sit.

Brody stood.

"And if you made some money you might help your own daughter out sometime, instead of leaving it all up to Charlotte. You might actually be of use to someone."

For thousands upon thousands of years men lived by their physical strength and talent, and now, suddenly, this. Slobs in designer jackets rule the world from mobile phones. Nothing but a disembodied voice ordering the troops of paper pushers: buy this, build that. Standing tall, looking down on Brody, Jacob spoke before he could stop himself: "In the real world I could crush you into powder."

Brody's face showed anger no more than one or two beats. Then he shook his head. He looked as if he might laugh. "What?! You are one total...After I came all the way out here to this God-forsaken...."

Charlotte began very quietly to cry.

Brody took a step backwards. "Okay, Jake. I'm sorry. This is all my fault. *Mea culpa?* Right? I didn't mean to insult you. We just got off to a bad start. It's a tough business, these blended families. You know I have two sons, they're with my first wife, and...Look, I'm an asshole. Sorry. But I know I am, and that counts for something? The offer still stands. You want a good job, flexibility, and a good salary, you give me a call. You can make your imprint all over the West." Brody rubbed his eyes and sat down.

Jacob walked out of the Prairie Diner, lifted his eyes above the low strip mall skyline, and stared up into the sky.

There were footsteps behind him. He felt her hand on his shoulder.

He turned. "Okay. I caught it. I know what I said wrong, in case you're worried. 'In the real world.' I know *this* is the real world, and I'm not crushing anyone, much less your boyfriend, into powder. I probably wouldn't do it in the 1800's either."

"I know."

"On the other hand, I might."

"I know."

"In the real world he could buy and sell me twelve times over before breakfast."

"That's only if you went to work for him."

Charlotte understood. She had always understood. If she hadn't, everything might be different. She might have made demands, he might have made concessions. He remembered a clear starry night, when they had been camping and sleeping in the open, on blankets rough as twine. She lay beside him, and he couldn't see her. But her voice held such conviction: "You have this bright brilliant thing, this talent for seeing how people really were, and how they are. When you channel it, it's like lightening made liquid, pouring the direction you designed for it. You're the type who could lead a cult, or found a religion, or guide a country through war. Don't change."

And he didn't. But perhaps he had. Her eyes told him he had.

She looked away, and spoke. "Go home. I'm sorry."

Sometimes, when Kate or Jacob would ask him, the guard would turn out the security lights at the Township, just for an hour or so. In darkness you couldn't see the distant parking lot, and the signs were obscured for the restrooms and the gift shop and the carriage rides. The Township moved farther back in time when the lights were out.

Jacob walked toward the guard station, and the man inside, Trevain, nodded and blinked off the lights when he saw Jacob coming. Jacob walked through the darkness, gradually adjusting to the light of the high bright moon. It was dead silent. Behind him the lights of the town dimmed the stars, so Jacob carefully faced ahead. He walked past the stables, and spoke softly to Diamond and Grumpy, and stroked their noses. He rubbed the stable cat, Washington, behind the ears. He passed his own station, and could barely see the rail that kept the tourists out of his workspace.

He walked to the garden patch where Mrs. Morris grew fresh

herbs, then around toward the chicken coop, where a fat lot of birds kept company behind the Inn. All were asleep now, including the tall gray-brindled alpha-rooster, who dominated the flock the way the biggest and strongest had done throughout the history of chickendom. This bird heralded each morning, no matter how gray and graceful, with a crow worthy of the Apocalypse. Jacob decided it would be good to have him in a pot, with carrots. Perhaps Charlotte would do that for dinner next week. No, perhaps Kate. Kate. Perhaps *Kate* would do that.

He could eat more often at the Inn, with Kate. That would save some money. His rent on the trailer was low, he had no television, no newspaper or magazines or health insurance. His only regular expenses were groceries, a little electricity, and a telephone. Now Brody was around, he probably wouldn't need the telephone. He would disconnect it tomorrow.

Walking the dusty path and inspecting his world, he saw himself with Charlotte. This vision fell on him sometimes. His imagination was so powerful that he would be convinced as he fell asleep that they were together, and he would awake with an ache that felt like she had died. He saw them in a tasteful little house that Charlotte had decorated. He was teaching history at the community college where her father was the dean. And Jacob saw Mabel running to him, felt her hugging him, the image sharper and more tangible even than the photograph he kept in his pocket. Somehow the idea of her was stronger than the knowledge of her existence. Just hearing "Daddy! Daddy!" in his mind was enough to make him stop, to grab his head, to collapse on the path and mourn. It had never been this strong before, never this bad. He knew being with Charlotte and Mabel was nothing but a fantasy, a beautiful lunacy, but it was so hard to keep it out of his head, to keep it from feeling real.

Jacob squinted out over the plane of prairie – a solid block of land meeting a solid block of sky in a straight line. No clouds, no wind. Still, the grasses moved, silvery pale. He straightened himself up. He needed to get moving before the security lights came back on, although he did not consciously acknowledge that this motivated him.

Jacob looked around at low gray buildings, empty, but alive, because they were used. This was not a ghost town, it was a community. This was his life. He walked to the front of the Inn, and looked up. There was a candle in the window over the door, sputtering low, flickering. Kate was still there. She was waiting.

Jacob knocked. It would be good to be with Kate, and then to rest. He had a lot of work to do in the morning. And he needed to talk to Kyle about making a chisel, to replace the one he'd given away. He was sure he was going to need it.

⚜ *No Place* ⚜

LAUREN COBB

I CLOSE MY EYES, CLICK MY HEELS AND CHANT, "THERE'S NO PLACE like home," but when I blink I'm still in Oz, Minnesota, snowflakes wafting down from the gray sky. Across the street old Mrs. Nygard peers at me through her spotless front window, and I'll admit I'm a sight, shivering on the porch in my flannel nightgown, my feet turning blue in ruby-sequined stilettos while Punch, our excitable half-grown boxer, squats in the snow. I want the dog to hurry so I can get inside before the school bus comes.

Punch does her business in the front yard because our backyard isn't fenced, and she isn't tall enough yet to leap over the front hedge. At last she shakes herself, and I totter down the steps in my heels to grab her collar. As I drag her toward the house, the yellow bus lumbers around the corner and wheezes to a halt in the middle of our narrow street. The bus driver sticks his head out his window, snow spattering his shaggy black hair. "You going to school like that, Jenn?" I cross my arms over my stiff nipples and shout back, "What do you think, Einstein?"

Running toward the bus, the Anderson brothers slip and slide on the icy sidewalk, their arms windmilling. Someone on the bus shoves down a window and laughter spills into the cold street. Cute freckled Lindsay Helquist and her friends crowd the window to point and smirk. They don't see the bus driver lob a crumpled paper ball at my feet.

Billowing white exhaust, the bus pulls away. I pick up the crumpled paper and haul Punch inside. She pads into the living room, circles the rug and curls up with deep sigh. Crouched in the mud-room, I fumble at the stiletto straps. My mom thinks I pull stunts like this to get attention, but that's not it. Like Dorothy, I need to believe I can escape my blighted circumstances, although in northern Minnesota I'm more likely to be carried off by a tornado than a pair of ruby slippers.

I pull on my mukluks and go into the kitchen to stand on the floor vent, breathing in the smells of biscuits, bacon and coffee. When I came downstairs earlier, Mom was at the kitchen table, wearing the butterfly-print scrubs she favors—like she's a dental hygienist rather than a lowly receptionist. Loose strands already slipping from her hairpins, she watched me over the rim of her coffee cup. "If you're serious about college, Jenn, you'd better stop ditching school."

I heaved a sigh. "You have no idea what I suffer, Mom."

"You don't know what suffering is, little girl."

Michael wandered into the kitchen then, damp hair slicked back from his forehead, gray eyes smiling. "Mom," he said in his sweet, gravelly voice, "can you borrow me five dollars?"

"Lend, not borrow." She patted his cheek. "Yes, I will. Hurry up with breakfast, and I'll drive you to school."

After they left, that's when I put on my ruby slippers; I just couldn't face another day in the walk-in freezer that's my social life. If only I were pretty, or sweet, or indisputably cool, but I'd have to check the box for none of the above. I have cumbersome breasts, dark beady eyes, pale frizzy hair and fat, chapped lips. Right after we moved here, a football jock asked if I was "part colored." When I said yeah, my grandma was half-chartreuse, he asked, "Is that an Indian tribe?" I flipped him off, but I still don't know if he was spiteful or just ignorant. Our dad always made a big deal about the difference between ignorance and stupidity, saying that the former was curable. He forgot to mention it's also contagious— I've watched Michael dumb himself down so he won't be shunned by the ignorant herd. Everyone talks about "Minnesota nice," but I haven't seen any.

While the floor vent's heat thaws my toes, I think back to the good old days last semester, when Lindsay and her satellites ignored my existence, before I had the brilliant idea for my social studies speech. Seeing the dead and wounded on the nightly news, reading blogs by Iraqi kids who've lost dads, uncles, brothers to the war, I'm infuriated by people who try to justify our invasion—doesn't anybody else notice that Osama bin Laden was in Afghanistan, not Iraq? That the whole weapons of mass destruction scare sort of…went up in smoke?

So I dyed a bed sheet black and sewed it into an abaya, then wrote a speech describing the war through the eyes of a teenage Iraqi girl. When I strode to the podium in my black robe, the classroom went quiet. Outside was a cold, brilliant December day. I stared at the blue sky and took a deep breath. "My father is an ordinary man, a shopkeeper," I said. "He's been imprisoned in Abu Ghraib for six months now. I wake up sobbing at night because we've all heard rumors of torture inside those walls. The Americans shock men's genitals, strip them naked to beat them with rubber hoses."

I described U.S. bombs exploding into houses, wailing mothers holding bloody babies. Then I looked straight at Lindsay Helquist. "An American soldier shot my cousin in the head. Tell me why you wear a yellow ribbon on your sweater. Tell me why you support your president's decision to wage war on my people."

Lindsay told me to shut up. Her boyfriend Billy Morgan threw a pencil at me. Someone called him an asshole and then people were standing, yelling, throwing paperclips and spitballs while Mr. Derkle hollered at us to sit down. A few kids took my side, but most shouted what the talk-show hosts call abuse. How did they loathe me? Let me count the ways—dumb bitch, towel-head, sand-nigger, traitor. I yelled right back in a cold pure rage that felt like silver fire. But when I glimpsed my reflection in the window—red mottled face scowling, the black hood slipping off my frizzy hair—I stumbled to my desk and kept my head down while Mr. Derkle "reminded" the class of our town's proud tradition of serving our country in times of war.

Now I'm no longer invisible; I'm a freak.

I was normal enough when we moved here three years ago, me a tender sprout of thirteen, Michael only nine. Like most tragic choices, it seemed a good idea at the time. My dad took a job as school superintendent so we could live in a small town and breathe clean air. That was before we learned that the pristine forests bristle with meth labs. Before I figured out that the other kids were swapping baseball cards and gossip in the womb, like their parents before them.

That first summer, a bald eagle carried off our Scottish terrier. The next winter Dad was driving home from a school board meeting when he hit black ice and slid into a tree. He died from head injuries that night. When we'd recovered some from the shock and grief, I thought Mom would move us back to Kansas City, where we have aunts and uncles and cousins, where my best friends Nicky and Jonathan live. But Mom got "romantically involved," as she calls it, with her boss, Eric Krueger.

He's an overweight Rotarian with more chins than an elephant seal. His smile gleams like a toothpaste commercial but his eyes are lake ice, dark gray and cold. So we stayed, and I went from being the superintendent's daughter to the daughter of that skinny blond making a fool of herself over the dentist.

My fingers are finally warm, so I uncrumple the paper and read a wrinkled message in black felt pen. *Come hang out. The white house behind Peterson's Package Store, top floor. –Patrick.* Wadding up the note, I pitch it into the garbage pail. Hang out, right. I'm only sixteen and he must be like, twenty-five. What a wanker.

I pour a cup of coffee and stand at the window watching snowflakes fall through bare branches. No shadows on the snow-covered ground because clouds have dimmed the sun. A squirrel flattens itself against a tree trunk, hide and seek. Exposed among the lilac's naked twigs is a bird nest that's somehow survived the winter storms. There's a poem in there somewhere, but I'm not going to write it.

I wander into the living room, flop on the couch, grab the television remote, and channel surf until I get sucked into a documentary on the Rocori High School shooting in southern Minnesota. They show a clip from that movie Bowling for Columbine—we're a trigger-happy culture, duh. When the documentary ends I kill the opiate of the masses. The blackening screen crackles like cat's fur.

Mom and Michael avoid Dad's study, but I do my homework at his desk, surf the web. After he died I searched for him in endless computer files of school district documents, household records. All I found were the first two lines of a poem. The first line said, *I love you like summertime.* The second line said, *Your eyes are my soft blue skies.*" By then Mom was already deep in love among the molars.

The computer's in sleep mode, a green crescent moon glowing on the tan keyboard. I shove the mouse around until the computer whirs to life, then log into my email account, stare at the empty white space of my in-box. Jonathan has dropped off the radar, and Nicky hasn't answered the message I sent her two weeks ago. She has a boyfriend now, does pilates with a girl named Heather. Trying to picture myself stalking through school in a black trench coat, hunting down Jonathan and Nicky, I type *columbine shooting* in the search box, click on a web site. The computer screen slowly fills with black text on a red background. Big letters dripping like blood announce *Columbine Paint Ball!* The text exhorts readers to *Re-live the experience! Enjoy this event to the fullest at our indoor Columbine High-School re-creation in Wyoming. Become a fearful student, a SWAT operative or a Trench Coat Mafia gang-member on a rampage and kill without mercy! Come shoot your friends and family in remembrance. Support our troops overseas and pray for them!*

Disgusted, I close Netscape. As stars hurtle through black space on the screen, my next brilliant idea arrives. At Rocori, at Columbine, those pimple-faced killers succeeded where my abaya speech failed. They brought the war home to us. I could do it, stalk through school with a paint gun spurting red globs on my victims. My moronic classmates would think it was real blood.

My backpack leans against the desk like a faithful dog. I dig out my notebook and favorite jewel-green pen to jot down my paint-ball hit list: Lindsay and her yes-squad, Billy Morgan, Mr. Derkle for giving me a C- on my speech, our Bible-thumping guidance counselor Cheryl Lindstrom. I write names faster, everyone who's ever jeered at me, ignored me, stared at my breasts without bothering to learn my name. I'll have to turn the paint gun on myself at the end, of course—a single squirt to the temple.

Michael has a paint gun and a Maxwell House coffee can of ammo, and I can probably scrounge a trench coat at the Goodwill store. If I'm lucky Red will be there. My favorite recovering alcoholic, Red constantly refines what he calls his system for living, which embraces everything from the ethics of mousetraps (survival of the fittest) to the art of eating well on five dollars a day. And he won't care that I'm ditching school.

Half an hour later, bundled into long underwear, wool socks, a sweatshirt, jeans and my parka, I slog downtown. The sky has cleared to patches of blue. An elderly man shoveling his front walk pauses to say, "Nice day isn't it?" I smile and nod, humoring him. At the corner of Yellow Brick Road and Main Street, a crow flaps down into the gutter and pecks at something furry, then flies off, hoarse caws trailing black wings.

Downtown is three blocks of stores, bars, and restaurants in yellow brick buildings. The Northern Tavern's neon sign glows above the Ben Franklin on Fifth and Main. Behind the plate glass window of the

China Kitchen a young woman sweeps the floor, her long black hair hiding her face. At the Goodwill store a cardboard clock hung on the door tells me the store reopens at two. As I wander down the sidewalk, the Oz patrol car turns onto Main, so I duck into Peterson's Package Store, walk straight through and out the back door. Across the alley is the white house where Patrick the bus driver lives. A staircase twists from the third floor's wooden deck down to the backyard. I see a calico cat sleeping on the deck, its tail a warm muffler over its nose. I stamp my numb feet, then pick my way through mud and melting slush to climb the twisty stairs.

Footsteps creak across the deck above me. I climb the last flight with Patrick the bus driver watching me. He steps aside, and I saunter over to the railing to gaze down on Main Street. A motorcycle rumbles at a stop sign. Red hurries toward the Goodwill store, a bobbing marshmallow in his dirty white parka. Beyond the town the sky stretches forever above flat green forest, the frozen white lake.

The cat yawns, rises, arches its back. I look into Patrick's dark eyes deep under his caveman eyebrows. "Why'd you ask me over?"

"It can't be much fun ditching school alone." He reaches over his shoulder to scratch his back, and his elbow juts up like a wing. "Come on in."

"What kind of fun did you have in mind?"

He grins and shakes his head. "Not what you're thinking. You just seem kind of lonely, like you could use someone to talk to."

My cheeks burn, and not from the cold. I shrug and follow him inside, shut the door against the chill. Windows filled with blue sky, a bleached wood floor, a futon couch, a rocking chair. I unzip my parka, toss it on the futon and sit down in the rocker. Without a word, Patrick walks through a doorway into darkness. A book sprawls face down on the futon, *One Hundred Years of Solitude*. Sounds about right. At the end of the room a doorway leads to the kitchen, dirty dishes on the counter.

Patrick returns with a small yellow jar. Unscrewing the top, he dips two fingers into the jar and bends over my chair. Menthol fills my nostrils. His eyes on mine, he rubs white goo on my chapped lips. I go still, wondering if he's going to kiss me, wondering if I'll let him. But he moves away and screws on the lid. "I've wanted to do that all year," he says. Great, he asked me over to heal my ugly cracked lips. I lean back and rock gently, gazing past him out the windows. "Nice place," I say. "How long have you lived here?"

"Since I moved to Oz, a couple years ago."

"How'd you end up in this one-horse town?"

"I liked the name." He looks around as if seeing the room with fresh eyes. I wonder if I want him to kiss me. He goes into the kitchen, comes back with two dark mugs of tea. The tea smells bitter, probably some nasty herbal concoction, but I clasp the mug's heat in my hands. He sits down on the futon, sips his tea, then asks what I've been doing with myself all day.

"Is this where you gain my trust before we get naked?"

He rolls his eyes and sputters a sigh, his masculine exasperation reminding me of my dad, who called me Goldilocks, laughed at my jokes, thought I was beautiful.

"I'm a grown man," Patrick says. "What would I want with jail bait?"

And not even pretty jail bait. He doesn't say anything else, so, haltingly at first, I tell him about my Iraq speech, how it made me a pariah, then the words come faster as I describe my plans for a paint-ball Columbine. When I look at Patrick, my tongue cleaves to the roof of my mouth. His caveman eyes are dark fire as he stands up and says, "You'd better go."

"Why? What did I say?"

"I was a bus driver at Rocori. The kid who got chased into the gym and shot? I went to his funeral. So excuse me if I don't appreciate your brilliant political metaphor."

When he opens the door, arctic air floods the room. He won't look at me as I put on my parka and stalk past him, huffy, ashamed and a little scared. The door slams shut.

By the time I hit Main Street, I'm pissed. Just to prove he didn't faze me, I prowl the Goodwill store until I find a brown leather trench coat pocked with cigarette burns. As Red folds it into a paper bag, he says the coat's too thin to wear around here except maybe a couple of weeks in the fall. When I tell him it's for a school project, his worried look fades. "I thought maybe you were gonna run away. Girls your age do that. They try to get out before these small towns eat them up."

I nod. That's exactly what Oz has done—my dad, my mom, my brother all swallowed here.

On the way home I stop at the Ben Franklin for lip balm. It's snowing when I leave the store. Dark clouds shroud the sky, and an icy breeze snakes under my parka. The light's fading, so it must be close to four. Mom will be home soon, Michael already there, alone with Punch in the warm dark house.

I do want to go to college, so I go to school for the rest of the week, enduring cold shoulders, eyes that look through me—an invisible girl walking down halls, sitting at desks. Even the teachers don't see me. When I get on the bus Patrick stares out the huge windshield.

On Friday Mom has a date with Eric. He sits in my dad's favorite chair, his multiplex of chins resting on his chest, plump hands on his belly twiddling thick hairless thumbs. I'm sprawled on the couch watching Pulp Fiction on HBO. When he glances at the television, his eyes are slits of distaste. I mute the sound and say, "So how's it going, Eric?"

He winces, but I'll be damned if I'll call him Dr. Krueger. "It's going," he replies. "How's school?"

I flash an insincere smile. "Terrific."

"That's good." His pale forehead creases as he tries to think of something else to say. I bet myself ten dollars he'll comment on the weather. He says, "Looks like we're in for a cold one tonight."

When Michael slides into the room, Eric beams at him. "Want to come ice fishing on Sunday, Mike? I've got my fish house up on the south end of the lake." As they talk about lures, ice augers and fishing poles, Eric shoots me a look, inviting me to see how well he and Michael get along. Mom comes downstairs in a red dress and black boots, so they must be having dinner at the Emerald City Steakhouse. After they leave, Michael goes into the kitchen, where I hear him on the phone talking about a girl named Ashley, making plans to go bowling with his friends. Maybe I should rob a bank, run away to Mexico or Tahiti.

Saturday morning the smell of sizzling bacon lures me downstairs. Mom's at the stove flipping pancakes on the griddle, crisp bacon piled on a plate, a pitcher of orange juice on the counter. "How do you want your eggs, honey?"

"Scrambled. What's the occasion?"

"I'll tell you in a minute." Spatula in hand, she goes to the hall and calls up the stairs, "Michael! Breakfast!" She waits until feet thump the ceiling overhead, then returns to the stove, cracks six eggs into a skillet and whips them with a fork, her other hand shaking salt into the eggs. A cholesterol extravaganza. When the eggs and pancakes are done she loads up three plates while I pour orange juice. As we dig in, Michael tells us about the eight-point buck Jimmy Goswell saw in the woods. That's when I notice the sparkle on Mom's ring finger. I push my plate away. "So Mom, what's with the midget diamond? Did Eric get lucky at the arcade last night?"

She blinks, and her mouth sags in hurt disbelief. Michael glances at her, hesitates, forks the last crescent of pancake into his mouth. While he chews and swallows, Mom holds out her hand, displaying the ring. "Eric asked me to marry him."

Michael stands up, slowly absorbing her words. Then he grins and kisses her cheek. "Cool. I bet he'll borrow me his snowmobile now."

Mom slumps in her chair, relief evident in her smile. Michael carries his plate to the counter, then thunders upstairs to prepare for the uncomplicated weekend adventures of a twelve year old. Punch scrambles after him, her nails clicking on the wooden stairs. Mom looks at me. "So, what do you think?"

"Snowmobiles are dangerous. People die in accidents every single winter."

"Everything's dangerous, Jenn. The icy roads up here, the traffic and crime back in Kansas City. Sometimes we have to take risks." She ventures a smile. "That's just part of living, I guess."

"I don't like the way Eric looks at me."

She leans forward, her eyes startled. "What on earth are you saying?"

I stare at her, bewildered, until slow enlightenment dazzles me. "Let's just say I'd never want to be left alone with him."

Her hand shoots out so fast I don't even see it. Her fingers grip my wrist, her other hand flat on the table like she's bracing herself to lunge at me. Her words hiss out low and flat. "If you're making that up, I swear on your father's grave I will never, ever forgive you."

The trembling starts in my hand pinned to the table, spreads through my body. I stammer, "Yeah, all right, I made it up. He creeps me out but not like that."

She rises, both hands flat on the table. I think she'll slap me or spit in my face but she shakes her head, releases her pent breath in a shuddering sigh. When she looks at me her eyes are empty. I'm not there.

After Michael and Eric leave for the fish house on Sunday, I hear bath water running, the radio playing. I hesitate, then go upstairs and knock on the bathroom door. Water sloshes in the tub, and the radio goes silent. "What do you want, Jenn?"

"I'm sorry, Mom. I just—" I bite my lip. I just what? Want things to be the way they were before we moved here, before my dad died? I rest my forehead on the door. "I'm really sorry."

Water sloshes again, and the door opens. My mother stands wrapped in a towel, her skin pink and slick with water. "I was so happy." Her voice is soft and wondering. She reaches out and smoothes my frizzy hair. "You tried to take that away from me. My own daughter. But you couldn't go through with it, could you?"

I turn and stumble down the hall. The bathroom door clicks shut. Lying on my bed, I trace the raised pattern on the thin chenille bedspread, white on white like a snow maze. I get up and stuff my hair into a watch cap. Grabbing the trench coat, I cat-foot across the hall to Michael's room. The Maxwell House coffee can sits amid the rubble on his dresser. I search the closet, holding my breath against the smell of dirty socks, until I find the Spyder Rodeo semi-automatic on a shelf. Luckily the instruction booklet is under the gun, and I sit cross-legged on the rug, loading red paint balls into the hopper, careful not to break their gelatin skins. The compressed air canister is heavy with Nitro, more good luck because I don't know how to fill it. With its long barrel and canister, the gun will be hard to hide, but according to the booklet the holes drilled in the barrel will muffle the shots.

The radio's playing Frank Sinatra through the walls. I creep downstairs and let myself out. Clouds cast a twilight pall. A car turns onto our street, tires whispering in the snow, headlights dim sparkles. Holding the gun at my side, I walk down the street without seeing a soul, everyone inside having dinner or watching football or praying or whatever they do here on winter Sundays. A few blocks from my house I raise the gun, aim at a silver minivan and squeeze the trigger. The gun's muffled crack startles me, but when red dye explodes on a side panel I grin, proud of my aim. I move on to Mr. Derkle's white garage door and wish I could linger to admire the splatter. Billy Morgan's house gets it once in the side, and our guidance counselor's porch looks like someone bled to death on it when I'm done. At Lindsay Helquist's house, I peer through the picture window at rooms lit by yellow lamplight, her family seated at the dinner table. Sometimes we have to take risks. When I shoot three bursts at the front door, the heads around the table jerk up. Someone stands and strides into the living room. I sprint up the street and down a gravel driveway to an alley, my arm across my mouth to stifle my laughter.

Downtown is deserted, all the shops and restaurants closed except the China Kitchen. In the alley behind the package store I consider blasting Patrick's house, but he's not on my hit list. Ducking through a gap between the theater and the bank, I reach Main Street directly across from a low building, Krueger and Walheim Dentistry. I take aim and let rip. Red dye spider-webs the plate glass window. I blast away until the gun coughs, out of Nitro. As far as I can tell, no one sees me walk home.

Mom's bedroom door is shut so she's probably napping. I stash the gun in the closet, unload the hopper's leftover paint balls into the coffee can, then realize that if anyone glimpsed the shooter, they'll remember the trench coat. One more trip downtown before I can declare this mission accomplished.

With the trench coat stuffed inside my parka, I sprint down an alley looking for a dumpster that isn't padlocked. The China Kitchen's dumpster is so full the lid won't close, so I bury the coat beneath slimy vegetables, soggy cardboard boxes. My head down, I walk away fast, but not too fast.

Michael's watching television when I get home. I ask about his fishing trip, but he just shrugs, his gaze glued to the flickering screen. Upstairs, I take a hot shower, then pull on sweats and crawl into bed, dialing my electric blanket up to four. When I open my eyes, it's dark and my mom's clattering in the kitchen, but she doesn't call me for dinner. After awhile I pad downstairs in my sock feet and heap a plate with spaghetti from the pot on the stove. In the living room Mom and Michael are watching Cold Case. Mom bends her knees to make room for me on the couch, then snuggles her feet against my thigh, so I know I'm forgiven. I eat spaghetti while the beautiful blond detective solves a grisly murder.

On Monday the *Oz Sentinel* runs a story about the paint ball vandal, but the grainy black-and-white photo doesn't do justice to the artistic spatter on Mr. Derkle's garage door. I go to school to avoid suspicion, and it's an ordinary day. I'm still invisible.

On Friday afternoon, I sit at my dad's desk and write in my notebook, *What I did was sneaky, the act of a coward. I should feel guilty but I don't. I'm glad I did it and thrilled that I got away with it. It's the only answer I can give the world right now.* I shut the notebook, slide it into my backpack, zip myself into my parka and head out into the cold. The snow squeaks under my boots, and the dark blue sky presses the black weight of outer space against the earth's thin shell of atmosphere. I don't know where I'm going until I find myself at Patrick's door. My heart thuds when the door opens. Barefoot, in gray sweatpants and a wife-beater, he looks me over. "If it isn't the paint ball vandal."

So again I'm sitting in the rocking chair in the sky flooded room, the calico cat curled on the futon. Patrick hangs my parka on a peg, then sits down and gathers the cat onto his lap. I don't know why I'm here, but I find myself talking about my mom's engagement, how much I miss my dad, how I've become a stranger in my own family. Patrick nods, listens. "Do me a favor," he says. "Meet me on the bridge down by the warehouses tonight, at ten."

"Why?"

"Will you do it?"

"Maybe."

He gets my parka, opens the door. "Dress warm," he says. I give him a wondering look, but he shivers and rubs his bare arms. It's time to go.

I leave the house before Mom and Eric get home from their hot date, then kill an hour at the Cabin Coffeehouse reading *The Things They Car-*

ried for my English class. Alicia and Lindsay come in. They glance at me, whisper behind their hands. Finally I step out into the night, relieved to breathe fresh cold air. Stars spatter the dark sky, which is faintly green as if the forest has seeped into the atmosphere. The streets darken as I near the abandoned warehouses, and the nape of my neck prickles with something that isn't quite fear.

The bridge rises in a steep arc over the railroad tracks, and a lone figure stands at the top. I trudge up the bridge and stop a few steps away. His smile glimmers in the darkness. He takes my hand and pulls me closer. We stand at the bridge rail facing away from town.

"Look." He points to the east where the sky shimmers green above the trees. The shimmer spreads into pulsing green luminescence. I tip my head back and see another green streak, then another. Gleaming and fading, drifting veils flow like mist, weaving a cathedral of emerald light above us. We watch the glimmering green streaks until our feet turn numb, our necks stiff, and cold seeps through our clothes. Patrick takes my hand again. "Aurora borealis," he says. "The northern lights. I thought they might be back tonight."

I touch my lips with my gloved fingers, hesitate, then say, "Do me a favor, Patrick. Kiss me."

Warmth leaps into his eyes, fades. "I'm twenty-six, Jenn. I can't take advantage of a teenage girl."

"You crossed that line when you asked me over to your house."

"Maybe." He turns to stare at the ragged pines on the horizon. "I'm leaving town at the end of the school year."

Night plunges through my heart's thin shell. "Where are you going?"

"No place in particular. It's just time to move on."

"Is it because of me?"

"Jenn, the world's a lot bigger than you." He smiles at my confusion. "It's got nothing to do with you. I just get restless if I stay in one place too long."

"Kiss me goodbye then."

"You ever been kissed?"

"No, well, once in the sixth grade, but that doesn't count."

He laughs under his breath, takes my chin in his gloved hand. "Your first real kiss. Sure you want it to be me?"

I stand on tiptoe, place a hand on his shoulder. His arms close around me. We look at each other, his dark eyes smiling, his breath warm on my skin. His lips touch mine, soft and cold, then wet warmth as our mouths open, our tongues slippery muscles. His breathing grows harsh like he's running from something. Heat flushes my stomach, tingles through my chest, and time slows like our car sliding through the icy intersection, my mom gripping the steering wheel not caring, just keep him alive, like bullets tearing flesh and lives, my dad in the hospital trapped under gauze and tubes. I push at Patrick's chest but his arms tighten, his tongue demanding until I shove hard and his arms slacken. Green radiance spills across the night.

Walking back through town, streetlights dimming the night's green sheen, we're ourselves again. He says, "This isn't such a bad place. You should give it a chance."

"Like go out for cheer leading? Or join the Lutherans? I hear the Wednesday youth meetings rock."

He laughs, gives my hand a quick squeeze. "No, you should keep on being your outrageous self, but maybe don't try so hard to hate everybody."

As we pass beneath the red neon glow of the Northern Tavern, I remember hiking in the state park with my father, the red and orange woods luminous. A warm breeze rained yellow leaves across our path. I think he was happy to be alive that day.

At my street corner, Patrick says he'll watch me home from there. Dark flames of desire lurk in his deep-set eyes so I don't dare kiss him again. I touch his cheek with two gloved fingers, then walk away, the air like ice in my lungs, the bare trees black as ink spilled on snow.

It's after eleven when I let myself in, and my mom is dozing on the couch under a blue afghan. "Mom," I say just loud enough to wake her. She sits up and rubs her eyes, frowns at her watch. "Where on earth have you been?"

"Watching the northern lights."

"It's not like you to just take off." She hesitates. "Is this about me and Eric?"

I shake my head. Now that he's oozed his way into her heart, how can I tell her that I loathe the thought of living with those chins, those thick twiddling thumbs and glacial eyes. That I fear what lurks behind his façade of Minnesota nice.

"You'll go off to college in a few years, Jenn. And Michael likes him." She sighs. "I need someone in my life, someone who makes me feel safe."

"I just wanted to see the northern lights, Mom."

She yawns and lies back down. "You should have left me a note."

"I'm sorry. I will next time."

"There won't be a next time, young lady."

But we both know that isn't true, so we say goodnight and I tiptoe upstairs.

Spring comes late in northern Minnesota. By the time the lilacs bloom, Patrick's gone. I'm lonelier than ever, but he gave me his email address, and sometimes he writes back. He's driving a school bus in Tilamook, Oregon. The way he describes the fog rolling in from the ocean, it sounds like a magical place. I save his emails, and sometimes late at night I read them, hear his voice saying that the world stretches out before us, our lives as wide and deep as the sky.

❧ *Bereavement* ❧

GREG HRBEK

His name was Rory. He'd been a late walker, a cautious boy who'd only recently taken his first steps when Mitch and Carolyn brought him to the lake in which he would drown. It still doesn't seem possible that he could've walked so far. Down the sloping lawn and across the full length of the dock. There have been moments when Mitch has doubted this version of events. He has actually contemplated the idea that one of his friends, or one of his friends' children, was somehow involved. This is how a cornered mind will lash out. If your baby can walk off the end of a dock and die in five feet of water, why couldn't one of your old college buddies be a monster, or the father of a monster? Thoughts like these provide a kind of relief. They function like a shunt, a metal tube driven into the skull to drain blood from the brain. Without them, the pressure would be too much.

He wants to try again.

Have another.

All along, Mitch has not wavered in his conviction that this is the best thing to do. The only thing. His wife doesn't agree. That's the worst part. Worse than the sadness and the guilt. It can feel at times like the entire world has been depopulated, like he and Carolyn are the only people left. Last two people on earth. Their course of action is clear. How can she *not* see this? She says: "You think we can re*place* him, Mitch? Even if we could— " But he's not talking about replacement, not in the sense that she is. She makes it sound like a pathetic delusion, like buying a set of bogus coins from a television shopping network. She makes it sound like betrayal.

"Not re*place*," he says.

"What then?"

He just looks at her. Glowers. Tries to express a distaste for her position so total it defies verbal communication. The truth is, he doesn't know what else to call it. He knows she's wrong, but can't prove the point.

"There's no word for it," he finally says.

"No word."

"In our language."

She pantomimes fatigue; presses two fingers to the bridge of her nose, as if to control bleeding. "What language, then?"

"Please," he says, not sure exactly what he's asking for. Whatever it is, the answer will be no. No replacement, no reminder. No more risks.

Fine, he thinks.

He doesn't need her anyway. Mitch would like her to be involved, but he's not going to wait forever. He's waited too long already. A whole year lost. Summer again, and the cicadas are filling his head with dry dizzy noise. Soon, his friends will be gathering at the lake, as they do at this time every year. It's not that he doesn't talk to them anymore. Just that the better part of their daily lives—potty training, nursery school, tee ball—makes for cruel and unusual conversation; and when it comes to the accident, to concepts like chance and injustice, the members of his brilliant circle, the philosophy and history majors, seem out of their depth. Mitch has tried. He has tried to discuss the thing dispassion-ately. Over the phone, over drinks in the city. His friends respond as animals respond to a territorial incursion. It's not him they want to keep away, just his tragedy, which might be communicable somehow. Fine, he thinks. He doesn't need any of them. He can get over this, he can mend what's broken by himself. Without telling Carolyn, he goes ahead and orders the kit.

Normally, you take a saliva sample from the inside of the cheek, send the swab back to the lab by mail, and receive, four to six weeks later, what is known colloquially as the "fingerprint." Hair, especially absent the root, is less reliable and not guaranteed to provide a clean print; but he tries to be thankful they at least have this. An envelope full of it. A souvenir of Rory's first and only trip to the stylist. If only they'd frozen some skin cells or banked the umbilical cord blood, things would be a lot easier. But Mitchell and Carolyn didn't save anything like that. Mitch had never heard of a cord blood bank. His grasp of science (he had once been told at a cocktail party) was roughly equivalent to that of a yeoman farmer. Well, he'd never had a mind for it. In high school, he'd barely passed biology, nearly failed chemistry, and weaseled his way out of physics. As an adult, he has chosen to ignore all these subjects, the way some people choose to ignore professional sports or the world of fashion. Carolyn's attitude is more actively hostile. She'll have no truck with science. When it came to childbirth, everything had to be natural. Having Rory was like starring in a reality television show about pioneer days. She delivered in the living room. No drugs for labor or pain, no doctors. Just a midwife, pots of hot water, and gore everywhere.

This is why he doesn't tell her about the kit. She would never understand. People's heads are full of myths and prejudice. Mitch doesn't fully understand himself. But he knows that what he is planning is no less pure, no less true than what happened in their living room that morning two years ago. Yes, you need a scientist to provide the code. But the code is not some artificial thing, it's not some pattern of lines on the side of a cereal box.

The code is *him*.

In a few weeks, the group will gather at the lake. Mitch figured the accident would end this yearly tradition, that his son's death would poison the place. No one would ever again want to assemble there in fraternity, mix drinks and barbeque steaks, play croquet, let their children on that dock, in that water. He figured they'd want to start over, somewhere free of guilt and ghosts.

He and Andrew discussed this a few weeks ago.

The two met at a quiet bar in the city and had one of those conversations that turned suddenly, needlessly defensive. But Andrew had started it by asking a strange question. Do you think you can ever go back to the house? Taken literally, the question didn't make much sense. The house belonged to Andrew's parents. Mitch knew them, but couldn't envision any event (besides, heaven forbid, Andy's funeral) that would ever bring them all together again. Maybe his friend was speaking hypothetically, philosophically, the way he used to. Mitch thought of times spent high and drunk as an undergraduate: imagine you're married, you have a baby and he drowns at my folks' house, could you ever go back?

"I could," Mitch responded. "Carolyn, I don't know."

Andrew nodded soberly, sipped his neat scotch. Then he said something about grieving, how people have different ways, different thresholds. He said he understood that this year might be too soon, but he hoped next summer. Everyone was hoping. Andy and Jamie, Rob and Jacqueline, Bryce and Lissa. The feeling was unanimous. That it won't be the same without Mitch and Carolyn.

"What won't?"

"You know, the lake."

Mitch was drinking mojitos. Though the day was not particularly hot, they were going down like Gatorade. He finished off his third while he tried to think of what to say. His head swam just a little.

"It just," he finally said, "seems so fucked up."

"What does?"

"Making plans. Like nothing happened."

Looking back, he can see how the words might be misinterpreted. But he'd meant no affront. He was simply amazed (he still is) by the persistence of life's patterns, how the world breathes in and out, without pause, no matter how much death gets visited upon it. He didn't mean to single out his friends. He breathes, too—and how surprising it can be to hear his own breath! Like when he wakes up in the night to a darkness so total that even sound and feeling seem to have been disappeared. Then from somewhere inside the darkness, very close by but at a great distance, comes the sound of respiration. A man taking oxygen into his lungs just as he always has. Breathing. As if nothing has happened. In this way, he is no different from any other survivor.

Mitch has to admit, when the fingerprint arrives (he gets it at work, where he has directed all correspondence from the lab), it does sort of look like something that could be scanned at a cash register. For a few moments, to object doesn't seem unreasonable. He has the sense, as he stares at the card—which is about the size of a wallet-size photo and shows a series of black lines, unevenly spaced and varying in boldness—that he is looking at something he was never meant to see. Mitch is not a religious person. But just holding this image, this information, makes him feel like he's offending someone or something much more important than himself.

The phone rings. He ignores it. Rings again. This time he answers.

"It's me," Carolyn says.

"Hello, you."

There's a long silence. Mitch knows what it means. He knows he doesn't have to speak. Just be there. A year on, and these wordless pleas for help still come regularly. He holds the receiver firmly to his ear while he stares at their son's genetic code. All at once, the doubt is gone. Time to stop searching for a middle ground. His family needs him. Sometimes, in the midst of all the sadness and disagreement, he forgets that he used to be a father. Passing a fingertip over the pattern, he thinks he feels a gentle shock, a tendril of static electricity reaching out from it.

He'll have to go to the lake. The drive will take about four hours. He could finish his business and be back the same day, but it's easier to explain a longer absence. So he concocts a story about camping. He excavates the tent from the basement, finds a sleeping bag in an upstairs closet, conducts a search for citronella candles. "Have you seen the citronella?" he says, feeling like this authentic detail should put him above suspicion. Carolyn stands in the driveway, arms crossed, while he starts the car. She looks forlorn and unconvinced. Mitch pretends to remember the kerosene stove. "Now where is that damn thing?" he says, standing on a stepstool in the garage, scanning shelves full of paint cans, motor oil, ceramic planters. He can feel her staring at him. He was in the clear and he had to come back for the stove. "Look," she says, "are you having an affair?"

An affair.

Mitch isn't sure who he is anymore, but one thing he sure as hell *isn't* is a lover. That, more or less, is how he answers his wife's question. Then he says fuck the stove and leaves. As he steers his car through the mountains, everything seems yellowed, aged by the haze of midsummer. Himself included. An hour later, he stops to call her, to say he doesn't understand these surges of anger, it's not her he's angry with, he's just angry. She doesn't pick up of course (she screens every call, rarely picks up, and makes no exception for him), but this is okay. The answering machine has become a kind of mediator, not just recording words but refining communications, brokering peace.

How did they get here?

The path is clear; but he still can't square who they've become with who they were, who they were going to be. Granted, he and Carolyn don't go way back. Just three years, to Andrew's wedding. Best man and bridesmaid. As the mateless members of the wedding party, they felt almost duty-bound to hook up, then after just a few hours started experiencing a sensation of kismet. They'd both crossed lately into their mid-thirties. They were tired of the singles scene, sick of renting not owning, afraid to be out of step for very much longer. They both liked kids and wanted one. God, the falling happened fast—and the baby came so slow. Month after month, it refused to take root. Then it did, but not deeply enough. After the miscarriage was when he got worried. Mitch wanted to go for tests; Carolyn wouldn't. Just refused, flat out. She wanted everything to be natural and organic. No treatments, no test tubes, no technologies. In the end, that's how it happened. They had good old-fashioned sexual intercourse and life began inside her and a baby was born right in their home. See, she said while their hours-old son slept on her chest, I told you it'd work out.

Now, in a way, they're right back where they started. There are times (this is one of them: alone in the car, deep in a world of trees, no sound but air rushing through the open windows) when it seems fatherhood was just a dream he had, and losing his son a nightmare within that dream, and waking life nothing but a stasis, a waiting, the painfully slow process of reconstructing what you thought was real.

He pulls up to the house around two in the afternoon. There is no car in the drive, no one at home. He figured Andrew's parents would be here. A sunny weekend in July. He's come prepared with a bottle of Riesling, ready to have a nice visit before asking their permission to take what he needs. He doubts their property extends into the lake bed, but he doesn't want to offend. Now he doesn't have to worry. He'll do the thing and they'll never be the wiser, and he won't have to feign interest in the trends and tumults of Mrs. Levy's three separate book clubs. A deep breath. Mitch can see, beyond the house, past a few stately elms, the water. Bright as a mirror angled at the sun and the sky. He gets the spade and the box of heavy-duty freezer bags from the trunk. Starts for the shore. On the drive up, he hadn't been sure what to expect. How many times, in his dreams and daydreams, has he imagined the accident?

Through the eyes of a god, through the eyes of his son. He's pictured the lake so many times. But to come back. To travel a great distance, to a place you've painted in the darkest of colors and see that it's still light, still bright blue and electric with sun glint. No evil, no killer to bring to justice. The water laps gently. Mitch removes his sandals, steps into the shallows. Minnows scatter. He sinks the spade into the bottom. Fills a plastic bag with wet earth. The substance is heavy and viscous, like fatty tissue. The more he digs, the more he gets on his skin and clothes. Finally, he just dispenses with the spade and uses his hands. As he works (packing bags, zipping them shut, and laying them on the dock) he glances at the house and the lake.

Fifteen years!

How many times that first summer alone (his major still undeclared, a first great love stressing a fault line in his heart) did he run headlong over these wood planks, wet feet leaving short-lived prints, to plunge into this water, this very *same* water? Stoned, drunk, lovestruck. Croquet at dusk. Skinny dipping. You scatter to different cities, but always come back; and with each visit the lake feels more like the most important place, the center, the heart of your own history. Significant others become spouses. Then, one summer, someone brings a baby. You still drink and smoke and screw, but the laws are changing a little. Is this the slippery slope everyone is always talking about? If you're the last, like Mitch, you start to feel out of place, like a kid brother tagging along on grown-up adventures, tripping on your untied shoelaces, falling behind. Is it inevitable that it happened, finally, right here? He remembers (it's a memory impressed on skin and nerves) walking Carolyn away from the tent and the music and the dancing, into the darkness, into a coolness that seemed to come from this water, the shore haloed with fireflies, everything wine-drunk, drunk on the promise of her.

"Mitchell?"

Shit, he thinks, looking up. Mrs. Levy has her arms crossed over her bosom; it's a vaguely compassionate posture. Mr. Levy, with whom Mitch has always had a shakier connection (ever since the time the older man discovered him, in the deep of the night, receiving oral sex in his favorite recliner), looks less sympathetic. He should shake his friend's father's hand, but his own is brown with mud. Mitch is knee-deep in their water.

Twelve bags of silt are piled on their dock. His face is likely red from cry-ing. "It's great to see you," he finally says. "I— I got you a Riesling."

It's one thing to gather the materials. Taking the next step, that's another matter entirely. Needless to say, Mitch has never done anything like this before. He goes down to the basement apartment (unrented now for the better part of a year), and stares at the eight pounds of mud stored in the refrigerator and tries to get up the nerve to lay it out on the counter and start shaping it.

What if he screws up?

He always has a hell of a time assembling things, even with instruc-tions; and he can't remember the last time he actually *made* anything. Carolyn's the artsy one. She writes poetry and once took a pottery class at the community college. Mitch is too prosaic for this kind of undertaking. He writes legal briefs and once had three training sessions at the gym.

They say the code is singular and infallible. It can only mean one thing; it can only produce one outcome. Hydrogen and oxygen, com-bined in a certain ratio, can only add up to water. Letters of the alphabet arranged in a given order will always make the same word. But water can be cold or warm, and a word can have more than one meaning. Right? Mitch has no idea if such reasoning is valid here. What's coldness or warmth but a feeling you get? What the fuck is meaning? Days pass. The more he tries to work out the questions, the less the answers seem to matter. Just bring him back. It doesn't matter if he's perfect. He doesn't have to be exactly the same. Every child has flaws. Every child changes.

Mitch reaches these conclusions on a Sunday night (sitting up in bed, viewing but not comprehending the football game) and decides he will do it in the morning. He'll take a sick day. Start first thing, right after Carolyn leaves the house. He always feels fresh, most alert and creative in the morning.

"Andrew called before."

"Who?"

"Andy. Levy."

The television is dark. His wife reads beside him by the light of a low-wattage bulb, not taking her eyes off the page as she speaks. He must've fallen asleep. Andrew. Mitch has been waiting for his call, dreading it, hoping his friend would exercise the better part of valor and keep his mouth shut if tempted to open it. Now Mitch shuffles into the bathroom, cleans his teeth. As he does whenever his wife is in earshot, he sits to urinate. In the last year, their marriage has been defined by this kind of timidity. They burn incense to mask odors. Dress for bed like people from another era. It's the middle of summer, and they both wear pajamas, tops and bottoms. When he climbs back in bed, he lies on his side, facing away from her and the light. Finally, she says: "He said you were out at the lake."

"I was."

"Doing what?"

He considers telling her everything. Thinks about asking, honestly, for her help. He could turn to her, look into her eyes. Maybe if they looked at each other, really tried to see, instead of always angling their heads away. But he can't make himself move.

"You didn't have to lie about it," she says, softly.

"I didn't lie."

"Hide it, then. Look, Mitch. We've both got our ways. There's nothing wrong with that. I just can't do it your way." He can hear her turn down the page of her book and close the cover. "It's like— it's like you want to make grief part of your daily life. Set a place at the table for him every night and just let it be empty."

"Not empty."

"No, I know. Not empty."

"I'd like to know what's so strange about that. You act like it's crazy to want him back." He shuts his eyes, hard. "Don't you want to be a mother again?"

There's no answer. He's not expecting one. The question has come to be rhetorical; and though he always asks it in a tone of honest inquiry, he knows deep down that his motives are egoistic. He doesn't know how else to change her mind, except through an appeal to her own self-interests. Because he hasn't believed for a moment this past year that she doesn't want their son back, wouldn't take him back if given the chance, or if forced into it. She's depressed. It's so obvious. But she refuses to treat this pain of letting go, the same way she refused to treat the pain of bringing him into the world—and as for the remedies of physical love, she's so frightened of getting pregnant again, she won't let her own husband finish inside her. So what is he supposed to do? What options does she leave him?

"It's like a maze," she says.

"What?"

"It's like a maze we keep getting lost in. You would think two grown people could learn their way through it."

He rolls over to face her, finds her staring down at him. It's an unnerving moment. He's not sure if it's the light or her posture, but she seems to be regarding him from a great distance and with a terrible intent. It's as if, while he was turned away, she ran from him; and is poised now to slip completely out of sight. It *is* a maze, he thinks—if he doesn't act, if something doesn't change, she will disappear into its inscrutable design and they'll spend the rest of their lives searching separately for the exit.

In the morning, he sits at the patio table on the back deck while she gets ready for work. Beyond the wooded interior of their city block, there are the monolithic buildings of the capitol plaza, which stand over them always, watchful and all-seeing; and closer by, on the fences that divide the back yards and gardens, the neighborhood cats, four of them, who also seem to be looking at him, judging him dispassionately. He is drinking strong coffee, waiting for the sun, getting that feeling again, the one he had in the office the day the fingerprint arrived. Mitch knows he has every right to possess the code. After all, he's the father, and half of it came from him. Still. He can't completely rid himself of a fear he's known, up to now, only in dreams. He can't figure it out. He can't see why what he's about to do should scare him in this way, the way he's scared when he dreams of having blood on his hands—but he can't deny the correlation. As if this too is a thing you do in passion and immediately regret, a thing you know not to do and can never undo once you've done it. He holds the coffee mug and stares at his hands. The first light, feeling its way through the leaves, finds every fine hair on his fingers, every crease on his knuckles, all the dirt under his bitten nails. From the street, the pounding heartbeat of rap music on a car stereo; from a nearby open window, the sound of a baby crying out in vain. When Carolyn touches his shoulder, he jumps as if at a gunshot, overturns the mug. "Sorry," she says. "Just wanted you to know, I'm leaving."

ꙮ ꙮ

Only after speaking these words does she see the double meaning. She didn't mean it that way, didn't mean to mean two things at once. But as she walks through the house then down the front steps to the street, trying to remember where the car is parked, she can't say that both meanings aren't true. She scans the block. No sign of her little hybrid. She is fed up with this shit. She wants parking. She wants the stupid city to issue resident permits; she wants a driveway; she wants a world without cars. She doesn't know what she wants. Left, she recalls. Halfway down Hudson. She remembers now, she got home late from the board meeting last night and had to park near the plaza, near the underground garage, in a violet light more unnerving than total darkness for the way it turns night into a stage where something seems bound to happen. Since the accident, she's been unable to decide. Is she immune to danger or does she carry it inside her like a pathogen? Nothing bad has happened in the past year, though it seems at every moment that something will. A highway crash that will put her in a coma, for example; or a tragedy much greater, some dark premeditated thing, touching her and countless others at the same time. Today, the anxiety is just about her, centered in her body. In her uterus, to be exact. If asked to explain herself, she wouldn't be able to. She just feels different there. Different than she felt yesterday. But she *knows* this feeling, this sensation that isn't really happening yet, this foreshadow of a feeling.

Not possible.

She's been taking birth control pills for months. Her ovaries are not releasing eggs. Her body, artificially flooded by hormones, thinks it's pregnant all the time. Even if her body is the one-in-ten-thousand that can figure out the trick, it's been a long time since there's been any semen inside her. Still, the feeling is so singular. Once you feel it, you will never mistake it for anything else. The joyful terror of something beginning, of a life-to-be, of life that is not yet living. No one knows, but this has happened before. Twice. Two times since the accident, she has sworn she's pregnant—and not without reason. Nausea in the morning; sudden storms of sadness forming over her heart; physical changes that are just uncanny. When she finally reaches the car (right where she left it, but wedged now between two sport utility vehicles), she starts the engine, turns up the air, then eases a hand inside her blouse and touches her breast. God, it aches. They've both swelled up overnight, just like the last time, and her nipples are secreting a milky fluid. She remembers reading about this in a baby book. The medical term escapes her, but the facts of the condition (a desire for, or a fear of, a baby so intense that the mind and body both come to believe it's there) are unforgettably bizarre. There's something wrong with her. Really wrong. She's not getting better, she's getting worse.

When Carolyn returns at dusk, she encounters the usual scene. The neighborhood children running up and down the sidewalk, weaving amongst the parked cars, chasing each other into the street. Tonight, she finds a spot near the house, in the heart of all this dangerous play. As she backs in (one of the boys darting behind her, drumming his hands on the trunk of the car), she makes eye contact through the passenger window with one of the girls, who immediately looks away, runs away. Carolyn knows her, or knew her. A year ago—when she was a mother, a blond mother pushing her blond infant in a stroller—you might have called them friends. For all the girls on the block, Carolyn had held a strange fascination. They flocked around her like disciples, called her name whenever she appeared on the sidewalk, inquired in reverent tones about the baby. Now sometimes they will wave sheepishly, but just as often they will avoid her, as if a parent has told them to. She kills the motor. Sits listening to the squealing and the laughter (which will go on until well after dark), then unclicks her seat belt. Exits the car. Locks it by key-chain remote control as she crosses the street. Can't stop herself, as she climbs the stairs of the house and opens the door, from looking back to see if any of the children are watching her. They're not. They're in their own world, playing in the street, attracting tragedy. It's a miracle they're all still alive.

Inside, she is surprised to hear the sound of the television; and to find her husband in the back room, wearing jeans, holding a drink in his hand.

"You're home early," she says.

He nods.

"Everything okay?"

"Sure, why?"

She shakes her head. "Good day?"

"Okay," he says. "Fine. The usual, you know. A day, like any other day."

For the rest of the evening, he drinks expensive scotch and gives off the aura of a bad liar. Nothing's wrong, he says. Office politics. But she's certain he never went to work today. How many days like this have there been? If only it was an affair, something as trivial as sex. But there's a different kind of secret inside him, as disturbing as the one she is keeping from him even now. Upstairs, she closes herself in the bathroom and removes the home test from its box. Urinates on the stick and waits. Negative, of course. What more proof does she need? Yet the hallucination will not fade. She needs to talk to someone. She has friends, of course, and none of them will understand. They're all mothers, all with living breathing children. Carolyn has nothing in common with them anymore. They say they can't imagine what she goes through. This is true. It's like trying to imagine what lies beyond the edges of the universe. Try again, they say. So earnest and innocent. Like it's a simple matter of calling for a stork. As for Mitch. How could she reveal this to him—that she has waking dreams about the very thing he wants so badly? She looks again at the stick. Negative. She should feel nothing but relief. You can't know what she knows and want to go through it all again. What if she lost another? What if one died inside her? After months, weeks, days. It doesn't matter when life begins. It doesn't matter if it's nothing but a clump of cells, doesn't matter what it is or isn't. This isn't about science, it's about loss.

Late that night (she knows without looking at the clock that it's late because the bedroom is dark, meaning the floodlights have been switched off at the base of the downtown skyscrapers), she seems to hear her dead son crying. Her blood catches fire. All at once, awake. Already propped up on one elbow. Listening. Mitch not in the bed, not in the room. The air coming through the open windows, stirring the gauzy curtains, is cool enough to make her shiver. Maybe a cat in heat, maybe a neighbor's baby, maybe just her imagination. Because nothing now. No sound at all. It's a summer night, she thinks. Regardless of the hour, there should be noise. Traffic, music, a quarrel in the street. Yet it's unnaturally quiet; and something about this silence, the way it wiped out those familiar cries, makes her eyes hurt. She gets up, walks out to the landing at the top of the stairs, where one of the wooden banisters still shows, in the form of several small holes, the evidence of the safety gate that was once affixed there. From here, she can see the front door (closed, its curtained window glowing with light from the nearby streetlamp), and she can hear the workings of the antique sunburst clock that hangs on the wall over the sofa. That's all. No other light or sound. Wherever her husband may be, he must be motionless in the dark. Passed out, she guesses, on the sofa below the clock; or still drinking, soundlessly, on the back porch. Time goes by, the way a river goes by when you stand on its bank—with a speed that's impossible to perceive until something, some floating object, ends the illusion of stillness.

There it is!

Not a cat, not someone else's baby, not a trick of the mind. This cry is louder and realer than the last, and seems to come from downstairs.

She does not want to go down there. This panic, this tearfulness. Same as that day at the lake. The same sense that something is happening which cannot possibly be happening. He can't be dead, he can't be alive. Carolyn tries to say his name. Cannot. Her voice is being seized in her throat. So scared, but she puts a hand on the smooth wooden rail and moves closer. She moves through the first floor of the house, switching on lights, searching for him, worrying that she's too late. That he's been crying for a long time and she failed to hear him. Even a few moments are too many. Just a few moments of unconsciousness, of self-centeredness. You can't look away. Never look away. Because it only takes moments for little feet to reach the end of solid wood planking and step off into the nothing of water. She can't find him anywhere. Almost every light in the house shining. But does she expect this light to make seeing easier? She turns them all off and stands in the darkness, breathing, trying to breathe. That's when things come clear. Not just a cry this time.

A word. Two distinct syllables spoken from below her, from under the wooden floor.

Mama.

She rushes onto the porch and into the night, then down the steps that lead to the yard. They have let it go. The area is thick with flowering weeds, which have choked the last tenant's perennials to death and given the little stone fairy (goddess of the garden, left behind on moving day) the air of a ruin. The apartment is faintly lit. The window blinds are drawn, but there's another window in the door; and when she looks through, she is unsure of what she's seeing. Two figures. One a man; the other not a ghost, not a shining spirit. No, whatever her husband is holding in his arms is made of solid matter. It's a baby and it isn't. It's her son and it isn't. If there wasn't movement, mouth making noise and arms reaching into space, she wouldn't think him to be living; if they'd buried a body instead of scattering ash, she might think her husband had been to the grave with a shovel. Grayish flesh, the color of unfired clay; features that are familiar but distorted and make her think not of a twin, but of a brother afflicted with some kind of chromosomal disorder. This is the terror she never wanted to feel again. He looks sick, like maybe he might not live, maybe not even until morning. But she's not too late! She's not too late this time!

Carolyn lifts her hand and raps on the glass and meets her husband's eyes, and becomes aware of an anger, fiery hot but so deep within her she can't actually feel it, she just knows it's there. How could he do this to her? Someday, the question will find a way to the surface; or it might burn out of sight and out of reach forever. The baby could live. They are at the door now, father and son. She can see him much more clearly and she is questioning her first impression. His flesh looks warm with blood, his defects nothing more than a trick of dim light. The lock clicks open, the door knob turns, the door moves on its hinges. Then he's in her arms. There is a disconcerting odor of natural decay, like wet fallen leaves or soft fallen fruit, but he's breathing, he's breathing. "Rory," she says, choking out the name, crying as she hasn't done in so very long. Not since that day at the lake. An outburst that seems to come not from her, but *through* her, as if she is channeling the sadness of someone else, as if there are emotions always struggling to make themselves heard from the other side, massing, crushing against the barrier that divides here from there, finding in people like her an opening.

❧ *Once* ☙

LATANYA MCQUEEN

MY MOTHER CALLED FROM ST. MARY'S HOSPITAL TO ASK IF she should pick the pudding or jello for dessert. It was the fourth time she'd called to ask me something like this. At St Mary's, the patients got to choose from menu cards what they wanted to eat for their next meal. My mother explained how she really wanted the pudding, but only chocolate this time. The vanilla made her want to vomit.

"Go with the jello," I told her.

"But I want the pudding."

"Then pick that then." I asked if she'd heard anything else as to how long they planned on keeping her. She said no one really knew and that she didn't want to talk about it. She brought up the pudding again.

"Sometimes it cramps my stomach," she said.

"You're going to have to make up your mind eventually. It's not like you have forever." I said it without thinking, regretting the words as soon as they were gone. She tried to ignore my comment by mentioning the talk show on television.

"I have to go mom," I said, looking at the clock. "I'll call later."

I remembered one night I went out for drinks with a friend of mine and his wife. We were telling stories and one of them said how, once, while driving home, he ran over a dog. He had been out with his coworkers having too much to drink, and wasn't paying attention when the dog ran out onto the road. He described the impact of the collision, telling me how he gripped the wheel to keep the car from swerving.

He said that afterwards he sat in the car not knowing what to do. From his rear window he could see it lying in the middle of the road. He knew if he went back and saw the state of it he'd have to tell someone. They'd ask him questions he wouldn't know how to answer.

He convinced himself there was no point in going back, so he drove away, leaving the dog to die.

"That's awful," his wife said. "It really is."

"Like you've never done anything like that before." Then he asked both of us to tell of something we had done. "Let's see, I'll give you another one. During my first job I spit in a customer's drink because he said I was going too slow."

"We've all done something like that. That's not anything to feel guilty about."

"Oh what is guilt but something to drag you down," my friend had said. "Give us another one."

"Okay," she began. "Once I told this friend of mine she was fat because she wouldn't stop complaining."

"That's not bad at all!" he laughed. Then he looked over at me. "Your turn," he said. "Come on, tell us, what's your once?"

It was my mother's lover, not my father, who took care of her. My father left four years ago, before any of this could happen. I imagined he'd be relieved now if he knew, being free of obligation.

It was my mother's lover who called the week before to tell me what had happened. He explained how usually he helped her to the bathroom. He'd put his arms around her and she used him as support to get up from the bed and to walk. He told me how he'd been in the kitchen trying to sort through what pills she needed to take and he hadn't heard her calling. He only heard the sound of her fall.

"She's not able to walk now?" I had asked.

"Well, sometimes I help her, you know. There's the pan, but she doesn't like using it. She says it makes her feel crippled. I told her there's no shame in using it."

"So what happened? Is she okay? Is everything okay?"

"Yes, everything's fine now," he said. He summed up what little he had gathered from the oncologists, explaining options carefully so he wouldn't have to repeat. "She's going to be at St. Mary's for a couple of days, until they figure out the best gameplan. Do you know the one?"

"Yes, I know it."

"I don't know why she just wouldn't use the bedpan. It would all have been so much easier."

"But it's not like it would have changed things," I said. "I mean, eventually it wouldn't have mattered."

"I guess you're right," he said.

Once, when I was younger, I stole a dollar from my mother's purse to buy a pack of gum. I had looked through her bag while she was in the bathroom, my hand rummaging through the packaged tissues and tubes of lipstick until I found her wallet. I had no money on me, and I figured she wouldn't care anyway.

While I was making rosemary chicken my mother called. Her voice was low, almost a whisper. She asked if I knew who Jackie Collins was.

"From *Dynasty*?" I asked. She told me that her roommate Edith's husband left her a couple of weeks ago for a woman who looked like Jackie Collins.

"I can't remember what she looks like. Describe her to me."

"Why didn't you ask Edith instead of calling?"

"Because, Edith asked me if I thought she was better looking than her and I told her no. I want to know what she looks like to see whether I lied or not."

"Where is Edith now?"

"She's in the bathroom, which is why I need you to be quick. Tell me what she looks like."

"I don't really know. She has brown hair, bangs I think. She's kind of old now. I think she was in *Playboy* once. Does that help at all?" There was no response. I heard her fumbling, and then the click of the phone.

The right thing would have been for me to go back, I knew this.

She asked me once if I would and I told her I couldn't. I explained how it wasn't the right time, there was too much going on.

"So when's going to be the right time?" she had asked, and I wasn't sure how to answer.

Once in college I bought an essay online and turned it in to my Philosophy professor. She had given the assignment weeks in advance, but I couldn't bring myself to do it. I paid forty dollars and when she finally handed it back to me, I threw it in the trash without looking at the grade.

It wasn't like I hadn't tried to be there. I made plans to, booking a flight to go back. I thought it'd be nice if I surprised her. It would also be easier that way if she didn't know; I didn't want her to have to worry about getting a ride to and from the airport.

The flight was for the following Friday afternoon. I left work early and took a cab to the airport. I only packed enough for a carry-on so I could go straight through to the terminal. When I got there they told me the flight was delayed, saying that there were complications with the plane. I overheard all of this as the flight attendant explained to the crowd standing in front of the help desk. The attendant told us it might be awhile, and there were restaurants around the corner. I went to Ozone-Bos and ordered a wine spritzer. As I sat in the lounge, I tried to look annoyed that I was there. I kept glancing at my ticket to prove that I was only here waiting for another flight.

But when I heard the voice on the intercom say that they were boarding, I didn't go. I sipped my drink and when I finished I ordered another.

Once, I rear-ended a car while backing out of a Mini-Mart. I didn't stay to wait for the owner to come out. It was barely noticeable and I was in a hurry.

It was my mother's lover, not me, who picked her up from St. Mary's. He was the one who called to tell me how she'd gotten to the point where she couldn't take care of herself. He said she'd be staying with him now, and called to make sure I had the right address and number.

I asked if I could speak with her and he said she was sleeping. His voice was strained, and I knew he was thinking about why I wasn't there, how instead I was over 3,000 miles away listening to the heaviness of his voice on the phone. Instead of asking, he told me that he got rid of the king-sized mattress in his bedroom to make room for a mechanical bed. He said he already hired a full-time nurse named Beth. He said that he promised her a Pomeranian if she beat it.

I wanted to ask him what happens if she doesn't.

At night, he said he slept on the floor beside her bed on the air mattress he bought. Sometimes, the thing deflated when he tried to move. He told me that all he cared about was lying there, listening to the sound of her breathing.

Once, I lied on a resume.

"You need to tell me something," I told my mother.

"Like what?" She was eating peaches on the phone. The doctors had given her a list of things to eat to help with some of the symptoms. She didn't explain the symptoms, but gave me the list of the foods.

"Like what's going on, what's happening. I want to know what's going on with you."

"Would it make a difference? Would you come?" She told me she had to go because she couldn't eat the peaches while holding the phone. "It takes too much effort," she said.

Once, I slept with a married man. He had picked me up at a bar that served peanuts with empty buckets to crack the shells into. He told me he was divorced and took me to a motel with a broken faucet and Impressionistic pictures of flowers and women sitting on lawns drinking tea. It was after he left that I found his ring on the carpet next to the bed. It had fallen out of his pocket. I decided to pawn it and used the money for things I didn't need.

I imagined what he did, this stranger who took care of my mother. I met him once over Thanksgiving. He made chili explaining how it was the only thing he knew how to cook. I ate it because my mother would have hated me otherwise.

It was this man who gave her the pills she needed to take. There were the drugs and the supplements, the pills for the diarrhea and the painkillers. Throughout the night he'd wake himself up, walking into the kitchen to take the pills out of their containers. He'd take the jug out the fridge that she loved, full of ice water so cold it was starting to freeze a little at the top. "Drink," he'd say, holding the jug while she took long sips from the straw. He watched as she tried to grasp the jug for herself. "Don't worry about holding it," he'd say. "Just drink."

I thought of the story with the dog often. I thought of it during the moments when I found myself waiting for the phone to ring.

"Thank god it wasn't a person," my friend had said later that night while coolly drinking down his scotch. "I mean, can you imagine?"

I should have asked where the difference lied between a person and the dog. I had wanted to know what it would have taken to make him turn around.

Once, I saw a woman fall on the street and I didn't bother to help her. I walked by without even looking in her direction.

"Mom, we have to talk. You have to tell me everything that's going on." I said. "I'm tired of this, you not telling me everything. I need to hear it from you."

"Will you come?" She started coughing on the phone, and then I heard a woman's voice, I guessed Beth, tell her she should drink some water. She said she was fine, told her that she wanted some privacy. "If I tell you everything, will you come?"

"Yes," I finally said. Then I sat down and waited for her to begin.

Once, when a homeless man asked me for change, I put a bunch of peppermints in his hand instead.

"Tell us," my friend had asked. "Tell us something we don't know, something you have done."

I heard the sound of my phone in my purse underneath the table. No one except for me appeared to notice.

"Well," I said, not sure how to answer. "Once—"

Once I told a great lie.

❧ *A Wedding Tale* ❧

BENJAMIN NOAM PEARLBERG

Ephraim Ben-Ari woke the morning of the wedding of his wife's friend with an ache in his back that reminded him of splintering wood. During a different period of his life when he once sat for thirty-six hours straight learning in a yeshiva study hall, he had heard that back pains were very much related to excess exposure to the sun and other sweat-inducing activities, like love-making and pitching softballs. Yet, upon reflection, Ephraim could not think of a moment in his most recent history when he'd subjected himself to such danger. Though not yet thirty, his life now was split between his dimmed study, developing a doctoral thesis which exposed the mathematical origin of gravity, and teaching physics at the local day school. He no longer trusted learned wisdoms from the years in yeshiva when his every waking moment was spent fawning over God and holy books. His religious passion, ferocious at age twenty, had long since waned and disappeared.

Sprawled across the bed and virtually immobile, Ephraim watched his wife as she stood before their mirror wearing nothing but the pearl necklace he'd given her the previous year for their first wedding anniversary. He watched as she slipped one leg and then the other through a pair of sheer white stockings, oblivious to the effect her naked body was having on him. Despite the fact many of their friends still viewed them in the romantic realm of a newlywed couple, the Ben-Aris had not made love in nearly four months.

Dalia Ben-Ari had dark brown hair which hung like a weeping willow, very much alive and majestically subdued with long subtle curls reaching down to her breasts, and it reminded Ephraim now of the way her hair had tickled his chest on their own wedding night and how in the dark he thought an assembly of ants was marching across their bodies.

At the wedding hall some eight hours later while he stood by the buffet table covered with steamed cauliflower and peppers and moist asparagus which made his eyes tear, Ephraim cringed from his throbbing back and marveled at how he'd been tricked into getting out of bed that morning.

It had not been the beauty of his wife standing alongside the bedspread, naked from necklace to knee, as he moaned to her about his pains. And he'd ignored her pleas for loyalty to the woman who'd been her best friend during the days when the two girls sat together each morning during prayers, making a pact in blood that they would see each other to their wedding canopies, be they separated by the ocean or sworn enemies. Rather, Ephraim Ben-Ari rose from bed that morning because his wife promised that the smorgasbord would break records not challenged in six generations since the wedding of the great Reb Shlomo of Snevyikov to the daughter of the community's sole physician (a bride whose intellect, it was said, was fair match for Maimonides).

"You don't want to be the one man in the entire province to miss the famed Leiberman shmorg because of a little back ache, do you?" Dalia said to her husband as she dressed. And that had been enough.

She was right about the food. Slices of beef thin enough to dimple in a spring breeze were transported on individual trays to the wedding hall by plush, refrigerated sedans. There were platters of steamed vegetables, mushroom and spinach knishes spiced in such a way that two of the bride's aunts spent the rest of the evening arguing whether the pastries were made of dough from the desert manna, or from produce smuggled out of Eden's garden patch. Legends took root around kebabs lined with sweet melon slices and chunks of salmon, marinated for exactly eighteen minutes in a wooden barrel lined with dried orange rinds.

The aura of stark young men standing aimlessly in groups of half a dozen or less holding china dishes that overflowed with culinary treasures did not fail to make an impression on Ephraim Ben-Ari. He thought it so full of humor it nearly made him forget the pains racking his body. For it was the presence of infinite excess mixed together with the very men taught to avoid it at all costs in all aspects of life (and he knew this well from his own lost time in the yeshiva circle when he was younger and, as he'd describe afterward, more impulsively romantic), that made him now imagine how they'd handle other influxes of material and physical excess: vats of red wines and obscenely curved sports cars, drugs of rapture, bordellos of women whose naked shoulders alone would have these boys crowing from the rooftops.

The groom during this time sat in a separate room at the head of three long connecting tables, each overlaid with an embroidered white tablecloth. He was surrounded by young and old men who'd already reaped their fill from the smorgasbord and were now singing and banging in tempered enthusiasm while they exchanged shots of whiskey and awaited the opening rituals of Yair Rotenberg's wedding.

Yair's neatly shaven face was pale from fasting and as time approached for the events to begin, little drops of sweat, like soiled tears, dripped from his sideburns down the edges of his cheeks, and he too joined in with the singing and clapping while guest after guest entered the room and came over to shake his hand, wishing *that from his loins and the loins of his new bride should spring the long-awaited messiah, quickly and in our lifetimes, amen.* To his right sat his father, and to his left sat the Chief Rabbi Eliezer Gold as pictures were taken and documents signed legalizing the proceedings that would take place in a short matter of time under the chuppah.

It was into this room that Ephraim Ben-Ari was drawn when the groom's mother and future mother-in-law were escorted to the head table in order to smash an earthenware plate against the back of a chair, symbolizing the permanence of the marriage engagement. When the women left and all documents were signed, calls for afternoon prayers quickly sprouted up with murmurs of *mincha, mincha,* cascading from the front of the room to the back where Ephraim Ben-Ari stood, passing lip to lip as the mass of dark clothed men rose and faced east to Jerusalem and her wailing wall. And it was now as he stood, silently muttering the mincha service which he'd long ago learned by heart but hadn't recited with any conviction in years, that Ephraim felt the first stir of angelic feet pitter-pattering in his bosom.

A true rationalist at heart, Ephraim immediately attributed this tremor to the mix of champagne and harsh whiskey he'd allowed himself to drink. However, in the back of his mind he could not entirely suppress memories from his late teens when his afternoons were meticulously scheduled around this same ten-minute mincha service, an impassioned date he'd made daily of love-laden praise and prayers. But this was as far back in his past as anything could be for a man of his young age of twenty-nine years, one week, and a day. And he had no intention or desire of sustaining such memories.

As the service concluded with the kaddish recited by a boy whose stringed tzitzit reached past his knees on either side of his body, and whose words echoed throughout the room with the soaring lisp of a tongue burned by coal, Ephraim Ben-Ari thought only of the pain that had progressed into several focused knots between the tip of his spine and points directly below his armpits. He was more preoccupied with finding a comfortable angle to stand against the wall than he was with watching the young men across the room take up a new chant as they lined up in rows of threes and fours facing the groom, arms locked across each other's shoulders like a sea of black netting. Nor did he take special notice of their escalating excitement as they prepared to march Yair to his awaiting bride for her veiling.

Ephraim watched the festivities with little enthusiasm. He followed behind as the groom was led toward his bride. He looked on as the rows of dancing men parted, allowing the man-of-honor passage and sight of his beaming wife-to-be clutching the hand of her younger sister who had deeper eyes and darker skin, and upon closer examination might have appeared a bit more flustered than even the bride herself. Ephraim saw his own wife standing among the bridesmaids screaming and clapping as Yair lifted up Shulamit's silk veil, and his wife's unchecked elation caught Ephraim by surprise and left him curious and unexpectedly wanting for a time when he too had been one of the bounding, screaming youths. But he quickly dismissed this feeling with embarrassed impatience.

🐦 🐦

In truth, the marriage of Yair Rotenberg to Shulamit Leiberman occurred once before. As teenage counselors at the Bar Kochba summer camp for the children of moderately religious families, Yair and Shulamit met and fell in love. They preached abstinence to their thirteen-year old campers during the day and practiced enraptured hand-holding alone in the evenings. Together, they felt assemblies of ladybugs fluttering across their arms and hands. They smiled at each other with pure thoughts and simple intentions, oblivious to any threats such affections had on their bodies or souls.

Post-twilight bedchecks of little girls and boys eventually culminated in a Sabbath-afternoon walk where Yair presented Shulamit with the black onyx graduation ring his father made for him upon completion of his high school courses. In full view of the camp rabbi and the newly bar-mitzvahed Eli Kessler, who was trying to understand the technical difference between acts forbidden and acts forbidden but allowed anyway (two unknowing, but fully legal witnesses), Yair placed the ring on Shulamit's finger, completely oblivious to the fact that, according to opinions of certain talmudic scholars, through this action alone he'd taken himself a bride.

Scandal erupted and spread precariously. Rumors of disgrace that would keep shameless grandmothers gossiping for the next seven years were initially covered up by hushed phone calls from the camp director's office to her parents and then to his, and a late-night arrival of a shaded van that smuggled the girl and her best-friend, Dalia Levine, back to the city and directly to the home of the Chief Rabbi Eliezer Gold. Upon arrival, the girl was taken immediately into the rabbi's study. Her friend was given a plate of stale pastries and made to wait by herself in the dining room where she heard only muffled cries escaping from the far side of the wall. And it was there, while picking impatiently at bits of a broken eclair, that Dalia met Ephraim Ben-Ari, the man she would marry in five years time.

"Are you the pregnant girl?" Ephraim asked upon entering the room, mistaking both Dalia and the rumor that was circulating through the rabbi's house. He wore the black suit pants and velvet yarmulke of a severe yeshiva student, and in his hand was a leather-bound Talmud tractate. He was tall and thin, his beard sparse, and he looked like he hadn't slept in days. Dalia was instantly smitten.

"No," she told him, and thinking of no easy way to explain her presence said simply, "I'm just a girl."

Ephraim, at the time a prized pupil of the rabbi's, was too distracted by his own spiritual crises having to do with faith and confused love for the divine to take particular interest in the pretty girl sitting at the table.

But a year later after he succumbed to a burgeoning boredom with the world of the fervently religious, after he left the yeshiva and terminated his studies with the rabbi, he would look back at this moment and wonder whether the girl really was as breathtaking as he remembered and, if so, how long it would take for him to marry her.

The Chief Rabbi Eliezer Gold was a man of knowledge and wisdom, and he took the example of Yair and Shulamit's accidental marriage as reason to condemn once and for all such mixed summer camps which encouraged nothing but immorality and licentiousness. An hour after their return to the city he had drawn up the divorce document which the Rotenberg boy was made to sign before the rise of the next day's sun as a precaution against any future accusations of bigamy involving either of the adolescents. Additionally, the boy was sent off to study in the prestigious, and highly rigorous Yeshivas Ohr V'Choshech, and the girl was made to meet with the Chief Rabbi every Sunday morning to study the rabbinical teachings of ethics and moral behavior.

So five years later, when a more learned Yair Rotenberg approached Shulamit and gave her the diamond ring that would begin their twenty-two month engagement, he made certain to stipulate that the ring was in no way meant to act as the equivalent of a monetary *prutah* needed for a marriage transaction. And as word spread of the upcoming nuptials it was the Chief Rabbi Eliezer Gold who certified that, "Nothing less than the love of God for His creations had brought together the once sinful Yair Rotenberg and Shulamit Leiberman in their redirected and penitent devotion to serving the Almighty."

🖋 🖋

After the wedding service, once Shulamit had circled Yair seven times under the chuppah; after seven rabbis blessed a cup of white wine officially infusing holiness into a ceremony that legally permitted Yair and Shulamit to satisfy their most physical desires; after Yair placed on her finger the gold band he'd bought the week before at one-six-hundredth the price of her engagement ring; and after he shattered a glass tumbler beneath his foot as a token of remembrance and mourning for the destroyed temple; after all this, while the newly married bride and groom were locked away for their first religiously sanctioned moments of privacy, the rest of the wedding party sat down to eat.

At the same time, the twenty-four piece band Arnold Leiberman hired for his daughter's second marriage began warming up on the stage of the grand ballroom. Mr. Leiberman had found the band through the first cousin of his wife's obstetrician, and he received a two-part guarantee in writing from each band member that they would: one, play a program of wedding music composed and inspired strictly and exclusively for his daughter and her new husband; and two, play their clarinets and trombones, trumpets, drums, French horns, keyboards, and tambourines with a fire and passion that could never be duplicated no matter how hard they tried or how much money might be offered.

Ephraim Ben-Ari sat beside his wife and watched the musicians as they knotted lavender sashes around their waists and began to tune their instruments with variations on a theme of crushed velvet. He was impressed by the fluidity and conviction of their finger movements. They reminded him of the resolve of summer rain, and without warning, sharp recollections of tenderness gripped him violently. For the first time in years he felt the curse of nostalgia his father had warned him about the morning of his bar-mitzvah when Ephraim questioned whether reading from the Torah would abort his childhood.

"It's not an aborted childhood you should be worrying about," his father had told him. "It's nostalgia." He spoke of it as if it were a lover, and this made Ephraim unexpectedly blush. "Nostalgia can arouse and soften the cruelest heart. It can lace the foulest piece of manure and make it taste sweet as a summer strawberry. But be warned," he told Ephraim. "You'd best stay clear. Nostalgia's dangerous. It kills quicker than a spoonful of curare. King David himself was stricken by immense nostalgia while he lay dying, and for this reason alone they brought him the virgin girl. And even she couldn't distract him! Stay away from nostalgia, it'll make the life you're living tasteless, and the life you've lived until now mouthwatering. Stay away, unless of course, you'd *like* to live your life eating horse-shit." And, even at the rebellious age of thirteen, Ephraim had taken this advice to heart.

But now, stirred by the wedding's mix of ceremony and romance, the renewed memories of excitement these events used to have for him, and the distance in time from when he'd last felt it as a participant; provoked perhaps by the pain in his back, the teasing chords in which the musicians were painting the room, preparing the guests for music capable of seducing fallen angels; or maybe simply out of longing for his own lost paradise, Ephraim began to sense the futility in his father's instructions.

The first course of hand-picked garden salad was presented before the bride and groom appeared, and Ephraim ignored it. His wife asked if his back pains were too strong for him to eat.

"At this wedding," he told her with a sudden and spontaneous vision which filled him with confidence, "one will either eat and drink, or one will dance. I will be among the dancers." He thought little of the pains twisting in his back.

And so it was that when Yair Rotenberg and Shulamit Leiberman were announced for the first time as man and wife at the ballroom's entrance, Ephraim Ben-Ari stood at the very edge of yeshiva boys waiting to whisk the groom away to the dance floor. And though Ephraim did not notice at all, nearly two hundred of the nine-hundred-and-fifty guests in the ballroom saw the bride's eyes harsh and red, and the groom's face a deeper shade of pale than it had been even under the wedding canopy. But having no certain ideas as to what had taken place in those first officially sanctioned private moments, and without a second more wasted away that might be spent dancing, the wedding party began its celebration with the overstated crash of a cymbal and an explosion of confetti.

Every inch of the five-thousand-square-foot dance floor was covered. Women formed multitudes of circles around the bride who danced in turn with her mother, grandmother, mother-in-law and then briefly, alongside her sister. On the other side of the floor, amid the hundreds of dancing men, and separated from the women by an unmarked, but meticulously-observed partition, Ephraim Ben-Ari found himself in one of the outer circles with his hands on the back of the man in front of him, and the hands of the man behind him on his own shoulders.

It didn't take long for him to realize the stupidity of the words he'd spoken to his wife. For, even though he was only moving at the pace of an old man, not doing much more than standing, the pain in his back was excruciating. Try as he might to control himself, Ephraim felt his eyes watering, and this further saddened him. Because he sensed not only decay in his physical stamina, but also a deep alienation from the world of this wedding. He felt an intimacy with, and at the same time, a dark distance from the man he used to be. A lone tear slipped down his cheek.

And it was exactly then that he felt the shiver of familiarity at a new touch on his shoulders.

When he turned around, what stunned him so completely that it shook the foundation of how he beheld his memory was more than the mere fact that behind him he saw God. What made his entire body itch and his tongue dry was more than the sight of God, and even more than seeing that God was a woman. It was seeing Her naked as a virgin bride that instilled in Ephraim Ben-Ari a most immediate fear of the Almighty. And while he quickly turned back and stared at the fibers of the black hat bobbing in front of him, not daring to blink, he felt Her hands digging into his skin, kneading each kernel of pain that gnawed away at the flesh of his back.

Only after several minutes passed did Ephraim build up the courage to speak. He told Her his back felt good now. And he felt Her breath in his ear soft like water.

Rising from mist of almost ten years past were recollections of a primal relationship existing between them when Ephraim believed his life would be dedicated forever after to this one love. It had been a puppy love, and he'd pursued Her daily, chiseling slow sacrifices of silent prayers that aroused in him fiery visions of Sinai. He studied Her always; memorized Her words, mouthed Her attributes. His naiveté in the realm of love acted as an aphrodisiac that had him lusting after Her demands for weekly goblets filled with red wines. Obsessions overtook him. Weeks were spent preparing Her bouquets of pomegranates and citrons which bloomed continuously through three winters. He saw Her only in his dreams and that was enough to inspire his fasts and provoke his songs in Her name, love poems composed three-thousand years earlier by a king smitten by the Creator. But even during that period, when his body yearned for Her as hard as his soul, and his soul gushed at every opportunity to serve, at no point had Ephraim ever seen Her naked.

And now, just as he felt himself aroused by the salacious presence massaging his back, he saw the band leader give his cue for the ensemble to bring this first set of dancing to its close. Despite his unvoiced cries for the music to continue, the dancers fell away, and soon the circle he was in dissipated, and as he stepped out from the dance floor Ephraim Ben-Ari felt the hands on his back let go.

Quickly, he turned around to find the beauty who'd burned through his dreams a decade earlier and whom he'd seen in all Her naked splendor only moments before, and to his distress She was gone. He was forced to watch, heartbroken, as the crowd of yeshiva boys and young women danced the bride and groom to their table set apart in the far corner of the room overlooking the river of the Lost Dove and its purple sky.

Seated once again next to his glowing wife, Ephraim Ben-Ari's thoughts circled viciously around the reappearance of his first true love, the cynicism that gripped his heart when She'd left him, the intricacies of their relationship that evolved once he started to question Her motives, Her belief in him, and finally, his own belief in Her.

"You look alive," Dalia told him, and her lips glistened from the fresh water with which a waiter had filled her crystal glass for the second time in the two minutes since she'd sat down from dancing.

"My pain is gone," Ephraim said. And he was telling the truth, for his back was healed so well he did not feel its existence.

"Good," his wife said. "Now you can really dance." And when she said this Ephraim felt a strange resonance in her voice, and he wondered whether she suspected what had taken place moments earlier on the dance floor.

The wedding until this point was, by all accounts, exquisite. Guests were too distracted by their own pleasures to notice the lone flower girl filling the room with a haze of colored soap bubbles in an effort to save what she alone somehow knew would be a disastrous celebration. Equally oblivious to what was about to take place, Ephraim fidgeted in his chair. He was restless and hot, and waited impatiently for the music to start up again despite the fact it had only just finished dying down. He watched the yeshiva boys and young women across the room as they arrived with the new couple at the table of honor, and once their singing finally came to an end, he saw the groom, exhausted and spent, take his place at the table and wait for his wife to do the same.

However, instead of settling herself in the satin covered bridal throne, Shulamit Leiberman took the skirts of her wedding gown in hand and walked to the platform where her father's twenty-four piece band was taking its first break. The illumination of generations of valorous women surrounded her as she ascended the platform and took the microphone from the band leader's hand. And while the nine-hundred-and-fifty invited and uninvited guests were scraping sterling silverware on stuffed chicken breasts, the bride asked for the attention of all in the dimming ballroom.

Like the rest of the guests, Ephraim Ben-Ari prepared for the first of what he expected to be many speeches and toasts in celebration of the newly-married couple. In fact, for the first few moments Shulamit's speech was ordinary in every way:

"Many people have come up to me and my husband throughout this evening and wished us mazel tov," she said into the microphone with a voice that flowed steady as the river beyond the ballroom walls. "And while I thank you for your kind wishes, this must cease. I am neither the recipient of good fortune, nor do I expect good fortune in my future. As for my husband, I believe the expression mazel tov is exceedingly inappropriate."

The walls of the room shifted and sunk deeper into the earth. Ephraim felt the water in his drinking glass freeze. From what happened next he would remember only the bride's one allusion to her husband's post-chuppah confession. "No mazel tov," Shulamit said, "for a man who walks through life without fear of God, a man consumed day and night with unholy lust! No mazel tov for the man who wished to leave me standing under the chuppah, but chose instead to save his reputation. Nothing for the man who long ago made a divorcee of me, and now promises to do so again. Only in books can you get away with confessions of love and lost love, Yair. But this is my life you've fucked, and now everyone here knows it!"

One-thousand-and-eighty-one sets of eyes belonging to guests, musicians, waiters, bartenders, and official ballroom staff turned to where the groom had sat himself down next to the chair meant for his wife of only two hours. But he was gone. In the hours that followed, rumors and accusations would attach themselves to four of the bridesmaids, the rabbi's daughter, a Romanian prostitute, and the bride's younger sister. Though little was ever confirmed, and the rumor regarding the rabbi's daughter highly suspect, the reality of Yair Rotenberg's transgressions was felt for miles.

On stage, the band-leader cupped his shaking hand around the bride's ear and whispered. He spoke for only a minute, but as he did, Shulamit's cheeks flushed and her dark eyes turned upward and she smiled. She raised the microphone to her lips once more.

"I have one more request," she said, looking out across the room at the tables of shocked guests. "Those of you who have faith, I ask only that when the band begins playing, you will dance. If not for my marriage then for me. Give me this night of celebration, make it mine. Dance for me with all your souls so the Lord above will erase this heinous marriage from memory."

And when the band-leader lifted his shaking hand once more over his keyboard signaling his band mates for the next set of music to begin, there wasn't a body in the room unprepared to take the dance floor in reverence to the shattered bride.

In a flash, the air swirled with colorful currents of chords in minor keys. Streams of music rolled from the mouths of golden trumpets and pristine clarinets in blasts and dribbles, bumping space with soap bubbles the bride's one flower girl had blown to prevent the very scene which had taken place moments earlier. The music battled the guests' memories of what they just heard for possession of their souls.

At first, Ephraim Ben-Ari watched with the hunger of a liberated voyeur. He watched rows of rabbis perform standing back flips in smooth succession while others slid across the floor beneath them. He watched the most serious yeshiva boys stamp the luscious dance of Yiddin with beauty and precision, a synchronous coordination that had them moving together as if attached by marionette strings operated from above by one master. He watched the men put forth all their energies onto the floor, spinning their shoulders and arms, kicking and jumping over each other's dancing bodies, twisting their torsos and legs with amazing direction and speed. He saw their motion blend with waves of sound the musicians were bestowing onto the bride in her prelude to a lifetime of suffering.

Now you can really dance, Dalia had told him earlier, and he realized once again how wise she was. The bride's words had touched him deeply, and he wanted only to dance in her name like those around him, to restore her honor. When Ephraim cut into the dancers and their coils of circles he didn't join in at the outskirts with the old men or even in the middle throng of swirling tzitzit strings and sweaty beards sucking air from the pockets of space between heaving bodies. He went for the innermost circle where the men danced with hearts borrowed from jilted lovers and felt each other's steps and turns with the clearest of vision only through sealed eyes. And here, with his first plunge into the madness of their dance, Ephraim Ben-Ari felt the return of Her presence he'd rejected and forgotten years earlier.

Her hands were on his back again, pressing, caressing, sifting his inner thoughts into separate compartments of loves, hates, and angst. The harder he danced the harder he felt Her crush against him, Her thighs on his legs. He saw the waft of flute sounds clearing space for him within the circles of dancers. Violins and oboes invoked a somber ring of cabalistic forests from the underbelly of Europe. And he danced into it with the spirit and body of his lover entwined around him.

Outside his forest, the guests were immersed in individual steps and half-steps that were momentarily robbing their minds of memory. The Chief Rabbi Eliezer Gold suffered the loss of recollection so severely he was assaulted by the fear that he was scheduled the next morning for both his circumcision, which had taken place eight days after his birth, and his burial, which was not to take place for another twenty-two years.

Only the bride was immune to the spreading amnesia, and her wound was so deep that her bridesmaids, who had now grown almost entirely stupid through their memory loss, inspired her to twist and stamp harder with each fresh song, engulfing her with their erotic screams and dances. But as hard as she danced Shulamit couldn't rid herself of the details of her husband's treachery. When the memory of each guest began to return, they saw the bride dancing amidst a growing pile of dust she'd kicked up from a deepening hole in the floor. And this only made them dance more rabidly around her.

At the same time, Ephraim Ben-Ari also danced with foaming ferocity. A sea of wet leaves brushed softly against his skin, and he had Her in his arms now and could feel the holiest of breasts firm against his chest. He wanted to ask if their separation was over, and She told him She was his to have. He had no thoughts of his wife, their marriage, or the four children they were destined to raise together. The beauty before him was too great. Her lush skin beckoned him with an aroma conceived to slay a field of bumblebees. Muted chimes and soft bells awakened his nerves without resistance. He remembered the day, lost like a sad nightmare in his past, when he last craved Her, and he felt the river outside hesitate and then halt in midstream. And right there on the dance floor, as Shulamit Leiberman was stomping her hole three-and-a-half feet deep into the ground, and as the band entered a phase of melody that made their sheet-music quiver, Ephraim Ben-Ari began making love to God.

He entered a cavern of endless space and perfect shape. Red butterflies fluttered around his hips, smoothing the dark hairs on his legs and thighs. Time stopped and moved aside, humbly making room for a force that gripped Ephraim with paralyzing light and blinding caresses. He felt his body moving against the rhythm of a deepening ocean. His nerves and senses were lost and confused, overwhelmed by inexplicable smells and tastes pouring across the surface of his skin. He tasted mango on his chest, smelled coconut through the tips of his fingers. His sex was surrounded and celebrated by flocks of serenading nymphs, until the physical pleasure was so great it grew irrelevant. And a delicious vision of creation swirled around him allowing him glimpses through angels' eyes of the world at its birth, nude. In every direction he felt Her glory as She showed him the history of the world in one overlapping moment. And then in a rush of pleasure and nostalgic sadness he was standing barefoot on hot desert sands, before the mountain, witnessing Her greatest revelation. His body shook spastically, submerged in exquisite and ephemeral warmth. And then it was over. And he found himself alone, at the edge of the dance floor, bleeding from the mouth.

With the completion of the wedding, the return of the bride to the home of her parents, the quaking of the community in its solidifying nightmare destined to tarnish its history for the next ten years (until the day a corrupt yeshiva drop-out would transform what had been an immortal scandal into a series of lewd jokes dealing with brides, incest and canopy beds), Ephraim Ben-Ari returned home. As he neared his house he could not shake the feeling that he and his wife were being escorted by a protective regiment of wild dogs. However, in every direction he saw nothing but darkness.

Hours later, when he woke in the middle of the night next to his sleeping wife, he was possessed to take down the velvet tefilin bag resting under a layer of dust on his dresser. And despite the fact he had once heard rumors of demons and hobgoblins that would settle with the permanency of ownership in the room of a man who dared put on phylactery straps under the light of the moon instead of the sun, he began to do exactly that. The cool leather tefilin wound itself around his arm and his hand and his head as if guided by a charmer's flute, and in the quiet of the night he heard the cantor's voice of a thousand and one prayers. As his wife slept, he held his prayer book closed between his wrapped fingers and swayed slightly to a breeze that pirouetted through the room. His mind closed, and he touched alternately, the tefilin box on his arm and then his heart, and the tefilin box on his forehead and then his lips.

When Dalia was stirred from sleep by his absence in bed, she saw him standing before the window wearing nothing but undershorts, the black tefilin straps wrapped around his arm and hanging from his shoulders, the square boxes firm on his body. She watched him, and she saw his lips moving. And she realized he was praying. And for a reason that was as unfamiliar to her then as it would be for the rest of her life, it aroused her terribly.

❦ *The Mean* ❦

MATTHEW PITT

Twenty after four on Tuesdays, the chimps went berserk. Their mayhem followed an arc (source, midpoint, apogee, to trace it on a rose compass). First the troop would pet at the safety glass lightly, as though consoling it. Then they'd prowl the perimeter of their cage, feet and knuckles skimming concrete. This was a warning, it meant their hearts were getting hotter, meant they were close to getting mean. They took their rage out on the bars. The chimps rattled the iron, clamping down, wailing to be let in on whatever secret it was outside that they could smell and hear but not see. Sometimes the head zookeeper would forget to put up their toys. That was when Tuesdays howled. The primates would hurl Wiffle balls, spinning tops, metal rattles, and building blocks at the bars. The noises were echinate, arrhythmic, and relentless. The chimps wouldn't let up for hours.

By then, Charles Shales and his high school students had killed their joints, cached their pipes, and vacated the hideout. By then they'd left the Milwaukee Zoo, gathered their paraphernalia, having taken pains not to leave behind any trace of their festivities under the scaffolding behind the Monkey House; they trusted the harsh winter winds to scatter the scent of drugs by morning, and the chimps' memory of the commotion to dull and fade. The group would ask Shales if he wanted to hang with them, but Shales would decline.

He'd have to come home and get his head unclouded in a hurry. Shales would have work to do in preparation for tomorrow's remedial algebra classes—maybe, say, a hundred papers to grade on the associative property—with a blue pencil and a bag of salt and vinegar potato chips as his only anchors. The high from the joints would be all but dried, just a small static gristle scatting somewhere in his head. But the pain wouldn't be back yet; that was the main thing. He figured he could barrel through most of his stack before the pain supplanted the pleasure.

After washing the skunk and zoo from his hands, Shales would pop in live tapes of Liddy's band, Some Assault. Would listen for her crisp drumwork, urgent four counts, and harmony vocal. He would bend over and tap his fingers against the speakers, head bobbing. The band was confident, brash, numinous.

They sounded—just as rock should—like polished hell.

The first ten papers Shales graded would actually be fine. But then he'd come to some kid who argued, say, that the associative property made every integer negative, once what was outside the parenthesis multiplied with the numbers inside of it. But this kid wouldn't call the process multiplication; he'd call it "claiming." He'd write for his sample problem: 1 (4 + 1) = -5, and then explain his reasoning: "*When the first one is claimed by the four and the other one, it's all bad. The first number is now a minus, and so's the second. Whatever number's are inside the parenth thesis have control over the other number. No matter how much bigger that other number is.*" And Shales would check the kid's name on the front of the paper and wince. "You're wrong in every way," Shales would write, "but you show your work well." He'd draw a C. Then a twinge would kick up, just beneath the skin. He would try not to look at the clock, mentally punishing himself when he took two glances in the same minute, wondering when Liddy would be finished with her show, when she'd slip into his room and climb in his bed.

☙ ❧

Wednesdays they held faculty luncheons at the high school. These were designed for teachers to relay disturbing student behavior, or to reveal any intimate grievances the students had confided. Usually everyone just swallowed their cafeteria food and left. The only real issue they wanted to discuss was, "Higher wages or we walk!" But they gave wide berth to *that* subject; the district superintendent was always in attendance, ass pressed against the radiator. Shales imagined that, at the first sign of teachers talking contract negotiations, the superintendent would press some button with his butt warning the governor and, that night, a midnight law would be pushed through the Wisconsin legislature declaring faculty luncheons off-limits to everyone but students.

After lunch Shales spotted Mary grading quizzes by the water fountain. He darted through the crowd to stand by her. "Hey Charlie,"

Mary said, picking sesame seeds from her undersized yellow sweater. "It's been many bells since we've been together."

Shales affirmed. The motor in the drinking fountain turned over. The other teachers filed out from the lounge, dumping their food trays. The smell of burned chicken patties wafted from the trash can just inside the door. Shales and Mary stood without saying anything. When Shales had first moved to Milwaukee, Mary had made overtures of friendship, had checked up on him. Since he'd gotten sick, most of their interactions consisted of long, desiccated silences.

"So," she finally asked, "how's your weekend shaping?"

"Oh, I can't think about that on a Wednesday." Any time other than the current moment felt far off to him. The weekend was an aeon from now; yesterday's high, the Pleistocene era.

She pointed to his eyes, which he must have forgotten to dab with Visine. "Looks to me like your weekend's already begun."

"Student papers. Can't get enough of the little geniuses. What about you? Are you doing something, going to a show?"

"No more movies for awhile," Mary laughed. "Not with 'the Spoiler' lurking."

"The Spoiler" was what the newspapers called Vondra Popeil. She had been haunting the Milwaukee Cineplex since midsummer, gaining notoriety and ire for standing outside the main doors and giving away the resolution to every new movie. "They get married, have two children. It's van Heuk who wrote the ransom note. Penny dies courageously, her mother gives up crack, they leave it open for a sequel." Since she was purchasing tickets to the movies, the police couldn't pick the Spoiler up for trespassing.

"It's too bad, too," Mary said, as if answering a question. "I could use more stories without endings. If she'd only cover my eyes and ears *before* each picture ended, I'd laud her with lilies." Mary was an English teacher, and Shales loved her turns of phrase. He loved how she could get words to do what she wanted—she probably didn't see it this way, but she'd tapped into a formula. She could create a little beauty with her metaphors and rhythms, a beauty that seemed to intercept the misery of time. In her own way she was preventing endings.

🜚 🜛

On the Thursday before the last Tuesday, Liddy came over to Shales's apartment after a bad practice. She was wearing a tank top with an iron-on peanut butter cup on the front. "I can't do this much longer." She clutched her hands, folded her knuckles—this was to work out the tension in her fingers. She gripped the drumsticks too tight, always too tight. "Charlie," she said, "you can only tell your friends they suck so many times before it puts the friendships in jeopardy…Maybe I should just give up and join the marching band."

He thought of her group, five of them, a prime number, indivisible. Then again, so was one. "If you join the marching band, I could come watch you play. In fact I'd get paid for it. But honestly? I hate pep rallies and the marching band gives me chiggers."

Liddy laughed and pulled off her shirt. Her breasts were rosy, the skin hot. She placed her arms around Shales, still holding the shirt. He could feel the fabric and the drying sweat on his neck. This was normal, he told himself, her coming over and peeling off her clothes. His listening to her discuss her career as a rock star while his cells tore one another to pieces like feral dogs. "So do you really want to do that? Quit? Don't you want the band to reach its full potential?"

"I am the full potential," she declared, rolling into bed. "My beat's the only good thing about us." She swallowed six pills, three shapes, four colors. Shales had asked her once why she never smoked with him. "Where you're going's good for you," she'd said. "I need something higher."

"So what was the problem tonight?" Shales asked. "Same as always?" Liddy thought the guitarist played like one of those solo-hogging dinosaurs from the seventies. "Jilt's really getting to you. I've seen the way you look at him the day after a show. Like he's stolen your best friend or your diary."

"I don't have a best friend," Liddy said. She darkened the room by pulling the sides of the pillow over her face. "Or a diary." She placed her hand in Shales's, into his grading hand, and let it lie. His lesson plans fanned out onto the floor. She'd be asleep inside of two minutes. It wasn't like before, though before wasn't so long ago: They wouldn't have sex, probably never would again, and this suited Shales, because when they did have sex he felt he had something to live for. It wasn't that it was so good, or so exciting. It was that it was irrevocable. No matter where Liddy went, what records she sold, or what shelters she wound up scurrying in and out of, she would remember him inside of her.

"It's not like Jilt's not replaceable," Liddy mumbled, more asleep than not. "It's his stash we can't replace. If he wasn't connecting us he'd be gone. I mean it, if what he was giving us wasn't helping you, he'd be a fucking antique."

She poked out from under the pillow when she heard Shales set the alarm clock. "Three hours' sleep. Can't you let me stay the whole night for once?" Shales ignored her bait. He wasn't going to get drawn into this argument again. They had agreed to these terms: She could stay over, but they had to get her out of Shales's apartment before first light, before his neighbors rose for the day.

❧ ❦

Friday morning before the last Tuesday. The oncologist greeted Shales warmly, not a good sign. His crinkled Midwestern accent was based on inverse proportion: The more dire things had become, the less urgent his inflection. It's metastatic, he said. It has spread to the liver. Does he want to be put on a list for something experimental? Or does he want to double the chemotherapy? No. To both.

The doctor's voice glazed over—grew so calm Shales wondered if he should expect to die this very moment. Shales has had breast cancer for nine months. He has been given an LHRH, administered cyproterone acetate, tamoxifen; chemo in tandem with CAMs; and of course the antacids, Alka-Seltzer, Tums, false trails leading nowhere. The only things that haven't let him down are the fat joints and the short nights with the seventeen-year-old stray who plays drums in bars. The seventeen-year-old he just dropped off, who by now is behind the McDonald's Dumpster puffing meth, killing hours until the school bus comes.

❦ ❦

That night Shales went to the Cineplex; *Hit and Run* was showing. In the theater he could smell chocolate being munched, could hear the parents brushing Kleenex below their kids' leaky noses. He turned and looked directly into the projector. By then *Hit and Run* had thoroughly annoyed Shales. Some facile load of bullshit he could've guessed even if the Spoiler hadn't screamed it in his ear earlier, where the rich girl and boy live fickle lives but learn about themselves thanks to the drifter they accidentally hit while driving their convertible; where the gentry falls on hard spiritual times but is repaired, ultimately, by this poor drifter who shows them how much they've been neglecting. When the end credits scroll, the gentry is more compassionate and the unemployed man has become the gentry's new caretaker, and there is a sense of justice, a sense that light rewards the lost.

The reels of his own plot was what Shales wanted to pick through, anyway.

On Reel 1 was Liddy—thin girl with dark-dyed hair, wet-looking like a tarmac after a rainstorm, knobby elbows, pale pink gums, small teeth that were sharp and told a story, tight stomach, trace of fat at the hips, wrists wrapped in white tape. The day of the first semester final exam, she'd worn a jacket with the McDonald's logo, a Taco Bell T-shirt, and a Jack in the Box necklace. She kept her bangs out of her face with a hairpin shaped like a carrot that had come from a juice bar. Shales approached her as he passed out ScanTrons. "I like the accesorizing." "Thanks, Mr. Shales." He had been Mr. Shales to her then. She had been the girl who kept dropping her pencil during the exam. Playing him for a fool, dipping down for quick peeks at a cheat sheet pressed between her sock and her boot. He told Liddy to stay after class. That was when she first called him Charlie.

Their conversation was initially gummy and awkward. I wasn't scheming, man. You were just dropping your pencil? Just dropping it. I drum, Liddy said. Beat skins. It takes a few days to recover feeling in my hands after shows. Against better judgment, Shales gave her the floor. She explained how good it felt, splitting time, or resurrecting it, as though it were dead, with booze and X buzzing in her at one on a school night. And Shales must have grown concerned and told her to go see a doctor, or at least the school nurse, about her hands. Then he must have slipped and mentioned himself. Mentioned, in passing, everything. He must have felt exhausted keeping secrets, must have been drawn to the prospect of giving away his secret, unburdening himself of it. Or, he was looking for another identity to climb into. He told Liddy he'd pass her if she wrote an essay defining the mean. She agreed and clasped his hand, and told him she was sorry about the cancer, Charlie, and there's something I can do for you, if you want.

Next Reel: Liddy gets on Shales's bad side. She doesn't show for a conference. He looks over her essay as the light outside weakens. Winter comes early in Wisconsin. She clearly has problems explaining math concepts in print. She thinks the mean is the number that occurs most in a given set. She's fairly bright, and he doesn't want to fail her, so he agrees to let her explain it to him orally. But she doesn't show, making Shales late for chemo. Shales decides on humiliation tactics. He takes out a Rolodex and calls Liddy's parents. A nightclub manager answers. He is amused to be speaking with a math teacher and is mentally recording every word Shales says for later tonight, when he'll retell it over a few cold ones. Liddy's the little wispy piece, yeah? Yeah, I think you've been had, teach. I may have three or four kids running around I don't know about, but Liddy ain't one of them. Parents? Don't think she's got 'em, truthfully. I think one died and the other dropped her. Beyond this I don't know, and since I'm not social fucking services I don't need to know, yeah?

Third Reel: Liddy walks in during conference hour the next day. High. Got my days confused, she giggles. I heard you spoke to Mom and Pop, and my uncle Jack Daniels. She giggles. I played last night and my head is still on nap time, so I guess you can flunk me. But Charlie, I really don't care. Last night we played great. I played great. I pounded so hard I couldn't say if it was the drumsticks cracking in two or my arms. She giggles. I'm no student. Fuck school, I'm a student of life. Too much life. Shales listens and nods, not with the consternation he thought he'd feel. The girl has guile, noise, and not a prayer of living past thirty at the rate she's going. She's his hero. She has talent—although most of that talent is anger, and will burn away as she forgets the family she is angry at. Liddy sighs: Am I expelled, Charlie? He rips her essay in two. I'll be dead inside a year, he says. That's an extreme. You live like Dionysus, that, too, is an extreme. The mean is balance. The mean is when both of us are sleeping. Any questions? Liddy says no, and Shales prints an A on her hand, on the spot where the stamp for last night's club is rubbing away. She pushes close to him and draws sticky, sweet breath on his face. I told you I would help you and I mean it. Can you smell this, taste this? This is what I'm good for. Prepare yourself, she whispers, for a little peace.

Shales found himself in the Cineplex parking lot, warming his Buick. He had no idea when he'd left the movie theater, or if *Hit and Run* was over yet. The car heater churned, biting into the accumulated sheet of frost. What if the Spoiler had approached him years ago, offering to tell him the ending he was living now? What if she'd told him that right out of engineering school he'd be designing Apache rotors to be peddled off to unconscionable regimes in shaky state-sponsored auctions? Or had told Shales that eventually he'd muster the courage to quit that job and leave California, where medicinal marijuana was allowed, for Wisconsin, where it wasn't, but only then would his body fall apart? Would he have believed her?

But there was no one to tell him the state of things, only X rays and biopsies…he was getting ahead of himself. Trying to finish the problem without showing his work. An equation was just a story condensed into one sentence, or a narrative in reverse. With a narrative, a reader waded through rows of flowery words hoping to come away with one core truth—with equations, a reader picked over the core truth, and then revised it, plugging in factors and numerals, deciphering, extrapolating, justifying its presence to make sure it belonged at all.

Reel 4 was Shales in transition, resigned to his desperation, letting it take charge. Reel 4 was when his view of life reversed: until now he'd been a disciple of moderation. He had tried to exist in the mean: meaning balance, meaning restraint, meaning a lapse in judgment in one thing—say junk food—could be remedied only by a stricter regimen in a corresponding situation—say ten minutes longer on the stationary bike. But as the pain intensified, all that sentiment broke down. Shales sought out extremes. He told himself he was still sticking to his philosophy; it was just his body was so wracked and torn apart that he had to respond in kind; the more apocryphal the sources the better. Shales tried support groups—a half dozen, until he forgot which building and which night and which of his peers were in remission and which metastatic. He sought out a therapist but couldn't afford it. He tried acupressure, shark cartilage, gin, and Dramamine, tried to take up the clarinet again, tried a whorehouse for the first time since the Army, tried mistletoe (which actually did keep him sedate through mild pain…could be just the act of chewing, or the unofficial theorem that enough shit flung results in some of it sticking). Then there was that night he drove over to Madison—on a recommendation—and was buzzed into a warehouse with an awful draft. Shales didn't remember it all, but the process involved having his head swaddled in a tunic, and resting his chin inside what amounted to a large rubber band suspended from the ceiling. He felt hands; they smelled of camphor; he heard chanting in French. All the while Liddy and her offer were looming, dilating, looking less crazy.

❧ ❧

So the deal went down. Liddy arranged to be caught with a note in class. Shales pretended to catch her and confiscate the note. The note was from Jilt, the guy who had the stuff, and it contained the details of the deal. *Meet at 2 sharp. You dick us you die. You squeal you die. You late you lose. Milwaukee Zoo. Monkey House. By the bush's. Don't look like a teacher. But don't look like a teacher trying not to look like one.* Shales tried to catch Liddy's eye to confirm these strange directives, but she refused to look up from her desk.

Shales left school before noon, feigning nausea in fourth period. He was sure it was a set up. He wondered if he should buy a gun at Wal-Mart. But he wound up bringing nothing but the hundred, in twenties, specified in Jilt's note. Oh, and wide-ruled paper, in case they had nothing to roll the pot into. Shales took back roads to avoid being seen, long and vacant roads in the industrial zone, Devore Drive, Jackson Circle Park, past the old cinema where he and Mary—before he got diagnosed—used to watch films together, past the alley behind the Pink Rink, closed now for six years, and so on and on.

It was bitterly cold but the sun was bright and feisty. He realized why this spot had been chosen. Sheets of blue tarp covered cranes and bulldozers: Construction was underway on the Monkey House, and the grounds were closed to the public. The area was abandoned. Shales stood in one spot, just behind a pile of pallets. His brow was moist and he felt more nervous than he ever had before a CT scan, or lying naked on tissue paper in some featureless examining room in Oncology. As he waited he watched his squat shadow lengthen in front of him, flatten, as though the sun were beating it submissively into the concrete.

The kids showed precisely four hours later, two hours late. They walked not toward Shales but past him. He didn't turn to mark their progress. A minute of silence passed, another, another. Finally he was sent for. Liddy emerged, took his hand, and led Shales beneath the temporary scaffolding in back of the Monkey House.

No one seemed happy to see him. Of course, he was the variable in this equation. They had all done pot before. They had been doing pot four, five, six years: as tagalongs to older brothers, at school dances to relieve the awkward roaming in the gymnasium, in bathrooms, in basements, in bed, taking a hit or two to help them relax before big exams. They had built this routine at the zoo—it was their textbook—and they were wary of allowing intruders in on the magic, especially middle-aged teachers in sweater vests. But Liddy had vouched for Shales and had, apparently, sweet-toothed Jilt.

Then Jilt reached for his inside jacket pocket, shoulders wide like he was baring his chest for the world. As he made these motions the group gathered round. Since there'd been nothing in the way of formal introductions, Shales listened closely for names: He knew Liddy and Jilt, Mikey had dropped out of his class the year before, there was the guy in back not speaking or being spoken to, and another one, either Claude or Claw, Shales wasn't sure which.

"You score kind?"

"Shit. Naw. DeJuan tells me like ten seconds ago he won't deal us out no more. Shit is that?"

"Shit."

"He try to up the piece's price?"

"Naw naw, check it out. DeJuan's a pussy, simple as that. Told me he cut out on school, cut out on dealing, all so he could work on his game at the yard. On his game—he's five foot *seven*. Can work on his game all damn decade, he's still gonna wind up just another unemployed nigger with a crossover dribble."

The quiet one, the one in back, looked at Shales for the slightest fraction of a second, to see if Shales was cool. Shales was cool. Shales was fighting pressure that was bench-pressing against his internal organs. He was cool with anything that would take that away.

"So then where'd you get the shit? Secondhand?"

"Would I fuck you like that? The shit is à la Ray's brother."

The dim thin eyelids rose. "Ray's *brother*?"

Mikey held his arms triumphantly overhead, bent at the elbows. "Touchdown!"

"Yeah yeah, but smoke good. Proceeds from this afternoon will contribute to posting bail. Ray's brother got DEA'd hard."

"Shitting?"

Jilt shook his head. "Real. They spun him, spun his house for six and a quarter. Spun dry."

There was a moment of silence to mourn the loss of Ray's brother to the Milwaukee penal system. Then the quiet kid approached his old teacher. "Shit Shales, this is your lucky day!"

The kid took a hit off something, and Shales stopped sweating. It was the first time in fifteen minutes they'd addressed him, and he figured if he didn't speak now, they'd forget he was here. "I don't know if you've been filled in on…what you've been filled in on. But I really want to try some of that…I'd pay…name your price."

"Name my price what *I* got?" The kid moaned ruthlessly. "Well now, let's see…"

"Kyle!" Liddy screamed. "He's a first-time customer. Just like anybody else. First-timers are always right; don't be a fuck."

Shales turned to Liddy, trying to beg her off. "But this is what I want."

Mikey grabbed Kyle's joint. "No, see, Shales, time to get schooled. This shit is just that, shit. What you want is what my man Jilt's got under the jacket. I'll translate it to math terms. Kyle's joint is addition and subtraction. Any penny you pay for that weak-ass, beaned, grown-in-a-tub shit is a penny too much. Kyle knows that, but Kyle knows he can't get high off anything anymore, and he just smokes for the recreation. What's in Jilt's jacket is logarithms and cosines. Hard-to-fucking-get."

"See what you want," summed up Claude or Claw, "is the kind."

Again Shales looked to Liddy for guidance, and got none. "I'm sorry. A kind? Kind of what? Kind of brand?"

"No," said Jilt, impatient at how long it was taking to hammer home the lesson, "the Kind." He pulled out the first sealed plastic bag and held it to his nose. "The Kind. You can't think about it this much or the shit won't feel good when you finally get around to doing it."

"Well, I have the money, old twenties, pre-1990, like your outline said. So can I buy some and…"

"We're waiting," Jilt said, checking his watch. "You should wait, too. You've waited this far for your hit. You might as well wait for 4:20."

"What's 4:20?"

The boys snickered, embracing the power of slang knowledge. "It's a special time. A minute we all hold dear." Later Liddy would clarify: 4:20 was ceremonial, teatime for stoners. Then she would step in before Mikey could take Shales's money to test the alleged Kind, and make sure they weren't beaning Shales. Liddy was his protein and his protector that first Tuesday.

Shales doesn't really remember the details anymore of the actual smoking; time wasn't passing, just sensation. Like the first time he'd had the courage to suck up all the way, and it was like he was breathing a garden. Or how Liddy's hair glinted under the sun, a color that couldn't have existed except in magazines or under black light—waxen, mordant magenta. The sight of mechanical lungs Mikey produced from his back-pack—"This is how you use a bong, man"—and how the smoke from the Kind he paid for waved feebly through the bong's chamber, like the hands of a man tentatively poking ahead in a pitch-dark cave. Shales's lower jaw muscles fibrillated between hits. He pinched his skin for the friction. The magic had come: It was now dullness in Shales's skull, not pain in his stomach, claiming authority. The dark pearled eyes of recon-noitering seagulls, settling on the zoo grass, a stopover on their way to Lake Michigan—the birds stood at their stations, tensed, and took slow, deliberate steps toward the humans, eyes surveying the sub-rosa scene point to point like Secret Service agents—filling him at once with both paranoia and peace. Come to get him. The monkeys hitching up their noses and moaning from within the cage. Come to get him.

After a few hits Shales decided to let himself into the conversation. The gang was talking about pranks—pulling the wool over authority's eyes, getting one's way despite the system, all that kid shit that really was cool. He would play it cool too; he wouldn't just start in. He'd just add a few *uh-huh*s or *right*s every now and then, until the others were comfortable with his presence. Then it hit him. No one was talking. They were busy smoking, or inspecting each other's skin for veins, or doing these things and looking at Shales. It was him; he had been the only one talking all along.

So it didn't bother anybody when Shales just started a new story, the one he'd been planning to say while busy listening to, and trying to politely interrupt, himself: "So I mean, just because someone's good with numbers doesn't mean they won't fuck with you. You know that Catherine the Great's math tutor, guy was Swiss, Euler, Leonhard Euler? Euler once tricked all these wealthy, erudite Court philosophers into accepting the validity of a higher power. Know how? Just wrote $(x + y)^2 = x^2 + 2xy + y^2$ on a blackboard, drew a line beneath it, and added 'Therefore God Exists.'" Shales drew in some more smoke; the old stuff was clinging to his throat. "So I guess what I'm saying," he said, giving everyone a moment to rein in their laughter, "is that this is really nice."

❧ ❧

After Catherine the Great he was in. The procession of Tuesdays followed. The kids were inquisitive, asking questions no one else in Shales's life had, or would. What was the Hemo-Vac like? Did it actually suck up blood? Why aren't you bald? How much time do you have? They began making sure he had better shit than the rest of them. They dropped their cost. Everyone wanted Shales's last hit of the day to be off their joint— they wanted something to remember him by. Shales knew all this—but he was getting more to smoke in the deal so he let it slide.

Besides, he was participating in the nostalgia, too. Watching how the boys stood, like cantilevered sculptures, one bent at the waist trying to cup a flame, another's legs sailing wide apart. Jilt, getting funnier and more confident with each week. Liddy was different. She was still beautiful but in the way of worn brick, not so much for her strength now as for her strength then. On the last Tuesday she was wearing houndstooth pants and Shales's Space Camp sweatshirt. She wasn't doing much at all, just packing on the vein leading to her elbow. It vaguely disturbed Shales that he couldn't bring himself to tell Liddy to stop. But she wasn't his kid anymore.

It was closer to say he was theirs. Now, it was closer to say this. They spoiled him. Mikey blocked the January, then February, now March, winds; Kyle patrolled the grounds more often—as the days lengthened, and the construction crew started putting in more appearances—so Shales didn't have to look over his shoulder. Jilt, like a grandfather, always had something special in his jacket pocket for Shales. The Tuesday episodes were feeling less like drug transactions and more like holiday reunions with family. Shales gave them updates on his treatment; the others stood and smoked and shot up, rapt, listening to him.

And Shales was astounded by their game of numbers. 1011, 808… Mikey can't make it today. Oh wow, why? 611. They'd picked up the codes of offenses from cops that had busted them, or friends of theirs. Rote memorization impressed Shales; he had a soft spot for attempts at order. Actually, he was prepared to call the group quite smart. They didn't possess dented vocabularies, just…specialized ones, for the benefit of their own comprehension only, all ties to classical expression severed.

"We gotta get nake sometime, baby," said Jilt to Liddy. He was playing with her, of course. By now everyone in the group except Claw (it *was* Claw) had slept with Liddy. Jilt was trying to get under her skin, but the only thing that could these days was the syringe—and bad shows, and when she heard Shales vomit from a bathroom or behind the forsythia that lined the Monkey House. Anyway the teasing was for Shales's benefit, too, to deflect the awkward silences. He was close to finished. He looked beaten even when grinning. His decline was clear to them all—maybe even to Shales a little less than the others. They blew out smoke but without much verve. You could hear the monkeys groom each other and hum through their flat noses.

Then Jilt said, "Man, we want to get something out." Shales looked up from Claw's bong. The circle tightened. Jilt cleared his throat and reached into his pocket. He pulled out a sheet of paper, looked it over, and glared. His ever-present smile went into hiatus. "It's wet."

Kyle: "What?" Jilt: "The page, dipshit! The page we wrote for Shales at lunch. It's fucking soggy!" Kyle: "Don't look at me." Jilt: "Who should I look at? Who else *had* to take a hit while we were writing and forgot to dump out his bongwater before he put the bong in my fucking pocket?" Liddy: "So just say it, Jilt. Say it to Charlie." A pause, because Jilt was collecting himself and one of the chimps had unraveled a hose and was whipping it into the safety glass. Quiet. Jilt: "Fuck. I forget every damn word." So they offered to walk around without Shales for awhile, and try to come up with a new page, but Shales did not want to be left without them.

※ ※

"In this problem, solve for *y*."

Shales stepped back from the blackboard the following morning, wiping chalk dust from his hands. He let silence take over. He watched the second hand on the hall clock sweep past twelve. He gave the integers time to sink in. Not one of the kids made a move for pencil or calculator. When he called on students for the answer in a minute, the faces would be blank and stiff, as though a military superior had entered the classroom. That was all just fine. Shales was rapt with two girls sitting in front. They were smacking gum—grounds for detention according to the rule he had floated months ago, when he cared about such distractions. The taller of the two girls had constructed a fortune-teller, one of those pinwheel-shaped puppets. She picked a number and used that number to guide her friend's fate, concerning who would ask whom to the spring dance. Shales couldn't stop watching. They'd written the names of two boys, Billy and Ryan, on all eight of the fortune flaps, and it was clear they had crushes on both boys. The whole thing riled him. Who were they kidding, giggling deliriously when they drew one of the boys' names? As if they were playing with chance, as if they had no idea how things were going to turn out. They were stacking the odds and pretending there was still something at stake. Look at them. Fingernail polish the color of grime, infantile light in their eyes. Giggling at their good luck. That's not probability. It's a mirage.

꩜ ꩜

Shales insisted on the Wednesday matinee. But neither he nor Mary were dressed for the Cineplex, which was kept uncomfortably underheated. So halfway through the film, Shales draped his arm around Mary like a stole. She let his fingers nibble below her left shoulder. Mary looked around. The screen was frightful and enormous. Though this was the movie everyone was hyping, and this was its premiere, hardly anyone was watching with them. Morning weekday shows were always this sparse, apparently: About ten ushers sprawled out along the back row, watching as spectators, and they seemed to be so comfortable as to forget they wore Velcro cummerbunds, or that their fingers were artificially buttered.

Shales and Mary stepped into the lobby. Shales took a long look at Mary, waiting for her review. "Well, you know, it wasn't bad," she offered. "But if I'm going to get fired for insubordination, I expect an instant classic." Shales thrust his hands into his pants, scanning the lobby. He seemed intense but in control. Not like the man who'd appeared in her classroom just hours before, who'd called Mary out of her room with a whisper. Who'd said he needed help, needed her, could she grab her coat and leave with him, right now? She could drive his car, he'd said, providing keys. There was no question: She could imagine him seized with pain on highway 94, car sliding over the yellow stripes, the road slippery with ribboned snow, on the way to Racine.

But then in his car he told her the pain was clearing. It comes, it goes. Shales asked if she would instead take him to the Cineplex, to see the matinee premiere of *Princely Sum*. And it was a good movie, just not what she'd expected. "What has that actress been in?" Mary asked. "Where I have seen her before?"

"Where is she?" asked Shales, stepping outside.

"That's what I mean. She absolutely rings a bell, but I don't know from where..." Mary looked up. Shales had stormed over to the box office window: He was screaming at someone there, a woman who had just bought a ticket. He was making wild, circling gestures with his arms, and his shirt collar fluttered as he wagged his index finger at her face. The woman cowered before Shales, ticket wrung in her hand. Mary stepped forward, peering in to the confrontation. "You dumb bitch," Shales said. "Listen good. Here's how it goes, here's how it ends. He doesn't get the girl. Okay? And when he slips into the coma? Slipping into the coma was the best thing he ever did."

The Spoiler stood quietly. Her face seemed tight below the nose, as though she were having difficulty clearing her throat. Her lips parted slowly, unspooling. Her ticket for the next show dropped from her hand and blew down the walkway. She chased after it.

Mary watched the Spoiler try in vain to snatch the ticket off the ground. But each time she had caught up to it, it spilled forward in the breeze, tumbling just beyond her tightened fist. Mary approached Shales, gazing at him: His teeth were clenched, his breathing abbreviated and heavy. Mary touched his hand—it was as if his heat had all coiled there. She began to laugh. Shales turned toward her, startled by her amusement.

"What, what?" she asked, still laughing. "What do you want, for me to send you to the principal? It was enterprising revenge!"

Shales wondered if he should let go of her hand. If he did, she would ask him to take her back to school. But if he didn't, he could prolong his day with her a little more. A pair of brakes squealed just then. An elderly couple had pulled their car over to the curb. They were studying the marquee, straining to read the show times, hashing out what to see, whether they would see anything. Mary called out to them: "It's safe to go in, in case you're wondering. No one's going to ruin your ending. We have this guy to thank for that."

Shales smiled. "Yeah. I mean, that's not why I came here." Mary studied her ticket stub as if appraising its future worth. "You have to believe that. Whew. For a guy with nothing left, I feel pretty clear."

"Well bravo, and I mean that. But your summary was shaky, Charlie. What film were you watching in there? He *did* get the girl."

Not the one he thought he would, and not the way he thought he'd get her. But somebody should be getting something in the picture.

Shales did the math. He considered his will, funeral arrangements, not yet finalized. It wasn't like it wasn't his body to do with as he wished. He didn't have to put his family's concerns before his, just because that was the standard thing. Fuck the visitation. He wanted to be broken down, become something else. He could have himself placed in an urn, to be signed for and picked up and carried off by Liddy. She could take his remains behind the forsythia at the zoo to smoke up the ash, suck up a high, some clutch of pleasure to trap momentarily between her teeth and throat, letting him escape, ring by ring, through the lips.

❧ *Hideous Thing* ☙

SCOTT WINOKUR

Mom and dad had been arrested on charges of grand theft, forgery, money laundering, and tax evasion, three-and-a-half million dollars going to shell companies and non-existent vendors from mom's employer, Dionysian Systems of Sunnyvale, California. Lynn learned this in the hallway of the Lotus Blossom Nursing Inn in lower Manhattan, the telephone wedged between her chin and shoulder to free her left hand, which Mrs. Wing insisted on holding—Jimmy Quan had the other one. Mrs. Wing and Jimmy Quan were two-hundred-and-three years old, together.

"They're looking at up to twelve years each and a million in fines, besides restitution," Nick said. "Mom asked if she could just pay it all back and they'd drop everything. Can you believe that? Aunt Connie's sure dad was tricked into going along. She wants his lawyer to get him severance. She got the idea off Court TV. They'll be out tomorrow on bail."

Hard to absorb—also to hear, above the racket on her end and static on his. Her brother was experimenting with down-market cellular phones from competing manufacturers, both of which wanted to go public. The hallway was filled with meandering wheelchair-bound residents, as talkative as they were demented; pacing ambulatory ones, mostly silent; Dominican nursing aides pushing meds carts and food dollies; and visitors stunned and repelled by the stench and spectacle of human decline.

"How'd you find me? I didn't say the home's name," Lynn said, loudly.

"When we lunched in Bryant Park you said you'd be spending Fridays playing Florence Nightingale or Margaret Mead or something with your Chinatown oldsters. You said Eldridge Street. Only a few nursing homes are around there."

———

Their last conversation, three weeks earlier, had been virtually all about Merrill Lynch's upcoming derivatives retreat in Westchester for promising rookie brokers. A very big deal, Nick said, and he'd been invited. As they were leaving, and he was paying with a brokerage-company credit card, he remembered to ask what she was up to. The usual, she said, her field work. He didn't inquire further, because, both knew, it would bore him. Lynn was in her second graduate year at Columbia. Her brother had a Wharton M.B.A., and NASD Series 6, 7, and 63 licenses.

Nick reminded her of Jimmy Quan's son, Ricky, owner of BMW dealerships in Jericho, Lawrence, Scarsdale, and Cherry Hill, N.J. Two driven charmers, smart and beguiling. Ricky wore fingerless black driving gloves and tasseled honey-colored loafers. He brought flowers and chocolates for the staff, said hello to the Alzheimer's patients like an old pal, and invited the Haitian janitor to sit behind the wheel of whatever Beemer he'd parked in front. He visited irregularly. His father had no idea who he was.

Mrs. Wing, in contrast, reigned from her wheelchair like the Qing Dynasty Dowager Empress. Her family came often and en masse, bringing dim sum, egg rolls, noodle dishes, and an ivory-and-camphorwood mah-jongg set, making a party of it. Mrs. Wing enjoyed watching others indulge, but wouldn't eat herself. She'd lived with a colostomy bag for ten years, since the week before her ninety-third birthday, and, far gone as she was mentally, continued to associate food with elimination. She closed her bone-gray lips against the mashed potatoes and puréed meats staff thrust at her and had to be fed intravenously to boost her red blood cell count.

Nick said things intended to buck Lynn up: good attorneys had been retained; any judge "with his head screwed on right" would see that there had been prosecutorial over-charging intended to please politically powerful firms in Silicon Valley; mom and dad had clean records and friends in the community.

"Do they? I can't think of anyone."

"Oh, I'm sure they do. We'll find 'em."

That was his way with his sister, who disliked his condescension, his fathomless confidence, and his swagger, but depended on him for certain essentials and was ordinarily too timid to complain. In a way, there had been no choice. Their mother was a histrionic terror, their father a frequently withdrawn depressive, their home variously an emotional wind-tunnel, desert, and Pinter play. Nick offered stability and optimism. He offered aspirin, water, and, literally, microwavable pizza, heat-and-serve canned food, and chocolate chip cookies when mom was too upset to cook and dad was in a funk.

"Which doesn't mean we don't have to prepare for the worst," he said before hanging up.

She'd been called Lin Yao ("beautiful jade treasure") by the nurses at the Wuhan foundling hospital where she was deposited in a straw basket twenty-three years ago, wrapped in white cloth. At her feet had been a small clay rattle shaped like a duck, her lone link to the unknown people who'd started her on the path of expulsion from her native world—charitably, considering their other options. By all rights, she should have been dead. Female fetuses and newborns in the People's Republic often failed to qualify as keepers under any circumstances. Those with an evident abnormality were at overwhelming risk for abortion or infanticide. And Lin Yao hadn't been normal.

She was renamed Lynn Ragusa-Cassuto by the newly accused swindlers—her adoptive mother and father, Lina Ragusa and Leo Cassuto of Menlo Park—on the flight home from the P.R.C. Lina was Sicilian in origin. Leo's family was Sephardic, from Turin by way of Lisbon and Tangier. Nick's tortuous birth had ruined Lina for further pregnancies, hence the baby shopping. Lina had been desperate for a daughter.

Ragusa devolved in the mouths of Lynn's brother and his friends to "Rags," a reference both to the Rágu pasta sauces that figured in so many hastily prepared, parent-less meals, and, less apparently, the tubular scar beneath her nose, which to a juvenile sibling suggested a stray chunk of spaghetti. Lynn, neé Lin Yao, had been born with a harelip, which craniofacial surgeons fixed up nicely shortly after her arrival in California, given the constraints of her condition and their craft.

She freed herself now from the bony grasps of the two moldering ancients, gathered her notebooks and tape recorder, and informed the head nurse that she had to go home, all the way to California. A family emergency.

"Hope everything's okay," the nurse said. "I wanted to hear about your research."

"Next week, maybe."

And maybe not. Twenty thousand dollars, at least, would be needed to make it to the end of the academic year. Her parents had been paying.

Lynn was in a program leading to advanced degrees in social work. Her interest was cultural variation in Asian-American and Pacific Islander-American eldercare. For an adviser, she had a faculty star, Dr. Judith Frank, who'd acquired a reputation on the basis of highly acclaimed books about Russian, Lithuanian, Belarussian, and Ukrainian immigrants. Frank spoke Russian, German, and Hebrew. She liked the fact that Lynn had been exposed in school and foreign-study programs to Mandarin, Cantonese, and Hakka, and had the highest hopes for her. Frank had to be contacted if she'd be away.

Lynn returned to her Chelsea studio, changed, and sat down at the computer. After reserving a seat on the red-eye to San Jose, she rose, and began to pack, crying loudly and copiously—a useful exercise she'd discovered for herself in times of crisis as a child. There had been family fender benders before—many of them—and several pile-ups (though nothing like this), but the things that had shaped her the most were the most forgettable and the most difficult to single out: the daily strife, the atmosphere of tension, the sense of being at the mercy of deeply troubled people. She'd lost trust long ago, and was by now nearly without a child's (even an adult child's) vulnerability. Her parents' arrest was another instance of Not Me, Not My Blood. Yet some intense sadness was unavoidable; you couldn't avoid caring about your parents, however much misery they caused, or fearing the worst when they lost control. So you vented. Then went on with your own life.

She sat at the computer again.

"Dr. Judy: I haven't found anything significantly different than what's been described by Tang at Berkeley and Chu's Case Western Reserve group. Patrilineal and patrilocal factors in most cases explain end-of-life placement and financial decisions, despite firm cultural and religious preferences for females in the earlier years of senior dependency. So what we are seeing is that the traditional Chinese belief that sons rather than daughters are necessary in advanced old age continues to hold, long after the abandonment of the rural lifestyle, immigration, and the attainment of financial security.

"My hope is that eventually I'll be able to show that this gender-defined pattern is artifactual, given that, in the U.S., females have legal parity with regard to property and inheritance rights, and presumably have similar resources. Therefore, new norms should be emerging. It's a matter of uncovering them.

"All this would be in addition to the secondary question we've agreed I'll address, which is the specific dynamics of the broad shift from family to nursing home as locus of immigrant eldercare."

Lynn fleshed out the message with references to "gender ideology," "survival strategies," "filial piety," "geriatric psychopathology," and "conflict between daughters- and parents-in-law." The obligatory buzz words and phrases. She closed by noting that she had to go out of town due to a family emergency and a business conflict making it impossible for her older brother to travel. She rose from her desk and gathered her toiletries, without shutting the computer. When she returned, there was a response.

"I certainly hope nothing terrible has happened, but it sounds like the OLD CHINESE WAY: girls go first when there's DIRTY WORK."

Frank's candor could be grating; also, her selective forgetfulness. Lynn had told her several times that she'd been adopted shortly after birth and that her family was Caucasian. But Frank seemed determined to believe that Lynn Ragusa-Cassuto was Chinese through and through, an extremely promising doctoral student steeped in the traditions of her homeland.

Lynn didn't answer.

Cassius and Brutus, the beribboned Shih-Tzus that Lina doted upon, feeding them New Zealand lamb and sending them to the groomer every Thursday, greeted Lynn maniacally—not a greeting, actually, but what they did: bark frenziedly, jump, chase each other, hump each other, and scurry away to the linen closet where they nested. Nick said the silly, rat-like dogs were gay. They didn't recognize Lynn, though she'd lived with them for years. Stupid, annoying animals; incorrigible nippers and yappers. Lina cherished them, like her other expensive accessories. Their topknots matched her outfits.

Great-grandpa Avrum's wall clock, made by a Porto horologist in the late 18th century, chimed in the foyer. Nine a.m. Lynn put down her suitcase and shut the door, a series of handsome grooved and dowelled oak slabs, inset with panes of thick faceted glass, and braced by flame-like bands of hammered iron. It had been shipped from Le Havre at a total cost of fourteen-thousand euros. Outside, on the semi-circular driveway, were her father's Lexus and her mother's Jaguar. In the garage, a 2,500-square-foot redwood building east of the main house, were a restored '53 Austin-Healey and an operable World War II-surplus Jeep. Above the parking space was a room paneled with cork and cedar and equipped with a Bose sound system. Lina used it for yoga and Pilates with private instructors, and weekly deep-tissue massages. The house, garage, and a heated pool sat on two-and-half wooded acres.

On the dining-room table off the foyer Lynn noticed a container of lotion, left by her mother. Lina was fanatical about hands and feet, hers and her daughter's. Manicures and pedicures, she said, were a "gift" a woman gave herself, a "reward." Scents of almond, lemon, and rose-petal balm always filled the house. Yet in all their years living together, Lina had not been able to get her adopted daughter to acquire a taste for similar self-indulgences, face makeup and lipstick, in particular. The problem was that nothing could conceal the malformation on Lynn's mouth—the all-too-obvious point of these degrading efforts. A man's voice rose and fell upstairs.

"I knew the stupid bitch was sending bogus invoices to Dionysian. I knew it was not legit. But she told me she'd stopped stealing the fucking money awhile ago."

In a lower tone: "I want you to know it was *all her*. I had nothing to do with this, Connie." Silence then, punctuated by one-word answers: "Yes," "No," "Unlikely." Connie was his older sister.

"She's already checked in," Leo Cassuto said after a long pause. "I assume she thinks it'll help with her defense...Well, *psychiatric*...I doubt it. This is a charade. But you can't *stop* her. You can't *tell* her anything. She sees what she wants to see...Yeah, sure. Separate attorneys, definitely...No, *I* didn't do anything. It was *her* decision to put the money in our accounts...Yes, it did go into our personal accounts, *but she did it*...I knew, but I didn't...Of course I should have."

He was quiet again, listening.

"Okay," he said. "I'll tell you when there's something new."

Leo sighed and hung up. Lynn heard him cross her parents' cavernous bedroom and open the creaky doors to the Arts & Crafts cabinet beneath the bay window overlooking the landscaped rear of the sprawling property. He kept brandy, sherry, and liqueur in it. Morning drinking, if that's what her father was doing, would be new.

She hadn't moved since entering. Was it a mistake to have come? What could she do now but bear witness? Nick had pressured her. No, he hadn't. Yes, he had—didn't he always? She lifted her suitcase and went out the door. It was ten blocks to town. She'd call a cab from there, return to the airport, and rethink the situation, then probably catch a flight back to New York.

But once inside Ida's, the coffee shop where she'd passed many hours in high school, the scales tipped again, and she phoned home. Guilt—"filial piety," if she'd been her own research subject—had won out.

Her father picked up after the answering machine went off.

"Hold on," he shouted, voice thick with suffering.

"Dad, it's me. I want to see mom. Where is she?"

"Why? She's a mess."

"Dad, where is she? I want to see her before I come home."

"Do what you want. Don't expect much. And don't be surprised by the crap you hear, even with the anti-psychotics she's taking. Los Gatos. Middlefield Pavilion."

Lina shared a room with a rape victim, a teen-ager who'd been beaten without suffering serious injury but was catatonic or shamming to a fare-thee-well. The girl slouched in a chair by her bed and stared at the floor. She wore jeans and a torn teal, black and white Sharks' hockey jersey.

Lina was a large woman with dark Mediterranean features and un-kempt black hair, heavy eyebrows, long, curling lashes, high cheekbones, and a dimpled chin. Long, scabby lines ran from her elbows to her wrists. Splotches of red-orange antiseptic and remnants of bandage covered both arms. Her fingernails had been cut short, and the polish on them was all but gone. She wore white institution-issued tennis shoes.

"Did you bring my Jergens? I left my Jergens on the table."

Her eyes were glassy, but Lynn still suspected fakery—she'd seen it so often before.

"I guess not," Lina said, adding, snidely, "At least *you* look lovely today."

"Mom, how *are* you?"

Lina turned away sharply, to face the window.

"Simply wonderful."

"These charges…What happened?"

"A series of tragic miscalculations. I should have gone to law school. I should have stayed single. I should have done this. I should have done that. But I couldn't do any of these things because of other people."

A familiar refrain.

Lina then shot a surprised look at her daughter, as if remembering something important, something it pleased her to talk about.

"You were a hideous thing when I laid eyes on you, *hideous*. It broke my heart."

Lynn drew a breath. She caught herself reaching for her lip. The remark, in substance, was nothing new, either. As a child, she'd trembled, as a teen-ager, smoldered, as an adult, gasped in horror at the source's viciousness, the subject's reflexive vulnerability.

Lina, her daughter was to understand, *wasn't* attempting to hurt her, to reopen wounds, to tear her apart figuratively, returning her to her perilous perinatal situation. Lina *was*, rather, trying to remind her of how far she'd come by virtue of her mother's great love, boundless energy, and unflagging commitment. Lynn was to understand this.

"So why'd you adopt me? Why not just leave?"

Lina exhaled, theatrically. Her heart was breaking, she meant her daughter to understand, but she'd speak, she had to, the time and place compelled it. Which was also painfully familiar: the straight-talk tactic, the usual response when in the past Lynn had chosen the wrong clothing, when her school performance had been less than stellar, when she'd failed to show affection or gratitude, when she'd done anything that prompted comparison with Nick.

"I wondered what would become of you, darling. I didn't want such a poor, pathetic little thing to, well, maybe to, to…Besides, we'd come a *very, very* long way."

"How do you know I would've?"

"Would have what?"

"*Died.* That's what you mean, isn't it? Or should I say, *failed to thrive?* I owe you my life, at least one worth living."

"You put it so extremely. But your chances weren't good, were they, sweetheart? Certainly you must realize that by now?"

Lynn's breathing quickened. She feared she'd feel ashamed any second. This wasn't why she'd come. But the momentum of strong emotion carried her along.

"I know you *wanted* a baby, mom. You felt you deserved one. That *had* to be a big part of it. I happened to be the only one available. There weren't any others for you and dad. You couldn't *get* them. The homes, the agencies wouldn't *give* them to you. They had *doubts* about you, isn't that right? So this was a *mutual* thing, wasn't it? You needed me as much as I needed you."

Her mother shook her head as if to say the last proposition was preposterous, unworthy of consideration.

"Answer me, mom."

Lina licked her lips. She wrung her hands.

"*Dad didn't care!*" she exclaimed, leaning forward. "Dad had a son. I did want a daughter, a baby girl. For myself."

She'd crossed her arms high over her chest and was clutching her shoulders.

"Besides—"

"And why *China*, mom?" Lynn persisted. "There were babies in the United States. Native American babies, black babies, Asians, white babies. You could've—"

"Your father didn't *want* a black child! He's racist. He hides it. But even if he did, it wouldn't have mattered. *You were all I could get!*"

Lina's voice was shrill.

"You can't imagine how *unfair* and *nasty* these agencies are, what they put you through, the interviews, the tests, the way they dissect you. And the money! Even when you prove how much you have, it doesn't necessarily work."

"Money?"

Lina crossed her legs, kicked off a sneaker.

"If they'll take it. Here they're picky. In China they have no problem. But they're greedy. Five thousand went to that awful home on the river, which stank from mold and shit. A thousand to a fat official with stinking breath and lousy teeth…and seventy-five hundred to the agency over here, which wasn't an agency at all, just a bunch of sleazy Filipino immigration lawyers in—where were they?—Daly City! Omigod! Daly City!"

She shook in revulsion.

Neither spoke for several moments.

"This trouble now, mom…"

Lynn stopped. Lina had an utterly incongruous smile on her face. It was jarring, like a clean white fungus sprouted overnight on a fallen tree.

"What's the matter, mom? What are you thinking?"

"*I was owed every dime.* This is the punishment Dionysian deserves. My boss was a monster. She made me take antidepressants. *So you people deserve it.*"

" 'You people,' mom? *Which* people?"

Silence. Scratching.

Lina looked out the window. There was a soft sound elsewhere in the room: the rape victim wrapping her arms around her knees.

"Should dad be in trouble, mom? Is that fair?" Lynn had raised her own voice. "Did he *do* anything? Or did he just—I don't know—*talk* to you? Or *hear* about something bad? Is it right that dad—"

"*Oh, he knows things*…I see what you're getting at. And I don't like being yelled at by my own child!"

Lina lowered her right forearm and scratched the obtruding vessels in it, as if the blood inside was burning its host.

"I'm told I quote unquote stole all this money," she went on. "I don't know about it, I have no awareness of doing anything *wrong*. But I'm not arguing, see? I want to return it and have the whole thing go away. I'm going to return it all, for chrissakes."

She threw out her hands.

"I'll give the goddamned money back!"

An aide passing in the hall stopped and looked into the room.

"Everyting aw ride dere?"

"We're fine," Lynn said.

When the aide moved on, she asked, "You still have it? The money?"

"What do you think? Do you have any idea how much it costs to—"

"So you couldn't, even if..."

Lynn let it go. Lina was scratching her thighs now. Outside, a Hispanic man in a white baseball cap began to hose down the walkway. Lina rose and knocked on the window to attract his attention, then blew a kiss. The man responded with a wary smile, parted lips revealing gold-capped teeth and a missing bicuspid.

"Before you leave, Lynnie," Lina said out the corner of her mouth, her face having changed yet again, to a masque of concern and determination, "I want to get a good look at your hands and feet. I'm afraid you're not taking proper care of yourself. Take off your shoes and stockings *right now*."

Lynn groaned.

"This is not open to discussion," Lina said.

Leo was dropping a partially filled black plastic bag into a garbage can as Lynn's cab pulled up. She paid the driver and went to embrace her father. There was no strength or feeling in his arms. He'd several days' growth of beard and smelled of alcohol. "I'm cleaning up—getting ready to liquidate. How'd it go with your mother?"

"I can't tell if she's losing her mind or just pretending."

"Why not both? I think it's both, but mainly pretending. She's shrewd and stubborn."

Lynn followed him inside. He collapsed into a reproduction Stickley chair in the den. The wall opposite him was covered with fair-to-good imitations of Sol LeWitt, Yves Tanguy, Roy Lichtenstein, and Lucien Freud.

Leo put his fist under his chin.

"So? What now?"

Lynn shrugged.

"You tell me."

"I can tell you what my lawyer says. I don't know what hers thinks."

Lynn got up.

"I need something to drink first."

"There's a nice sherry upstairs."

Her father was on the phone when she re-entered with a glass of water. He was scheduling something, and there was disagreement about the cost. He claimed he'd been told fifteen percent, but the person on the other end apparently was saying it was higher.

He hung up.

"This is all new to me." He laughed, queerly, eyes wide with amazement, mouth fixed in a tensed, unreal grin. "It's not every day you have to raise four-million dollars."

"Four million?"

"At least, including the legal fees. Probably more. This house, you know—or maybe you don't—this house is on the market. So's everything in it. That was the auctioneer. Gets a third of what he brings in."

"You're doing this because you have to?"

"No! I'm doing it for my health…Oh, Christ, I'm sorry…It might mean two years in prison, instead of twelve. That's how they've presented it to me…Sweetheart, you might as well know that you are *on your own*— you have been for days."

"You're not fighting it?"

"We have attorneys, but the reality is they're just trying to negotiate the best possible deal. The D.A. has us cold, even if your mother thinks she'll be able to convince people that *she's* too crazy to face charges, let alone to have planned and executed a complex financial crime."

"Maybe it's true."

Leo shook his head, emphatically.

"Something else: I'm getting another lawyer, a divorce attorney."

A short silence followed, then he rose, went to the bookcase, and bent to its lowest shelf. He withdrew a volume bound in thick red cardboard. In an upper corner was a circular portrait of Chairman Mao surrounded by happy workers. Mao's cheeks were apple red. The workers looked big, healthy, and athletic, like dancers in the "The Red Detachment of Women."

"You've never seen these. Mom hid them. I found the album going through our stuff. They're photos I took around Wuhan. We had time to kill. I went wandering."

Leo handed it to Lynn.

"Why didn't mom want me to see this?"

"Too depressing. That's what she claimed. Which didn't prevent her from threatening to take them out when she was mad at you. The pictures aren't good, but they'll give you an idea."

Hesitantly, Lynn opened the album. Only the first few pages had photos.

There was a picture of children, naked from the waist down, playing in a ditch. Another showed an elderly woman braiding garlic. Behind her was a rabbit hutch.

"I didn't know they ate rabbits in China."

"They eat everything, Lynnie. Dogs, cats, wild animals. Just hack them up."

Another page showed bleak dwellings along a tree-lined lane, most thatch-roofed, mud-walled, and very old. Some had small gardens and sheds for pigs.

There were photos of people doing farm chores (force-feeding ducks, hand-harvesting barley), and of Wuhan street scenes: a vendor ladling noodles from a steaming cauldron; a man bathing an infant in the courtyard of an apartment building; an old man sitting cross-legged while instructing a girl in calligraphy.

No one was dressed well. Adults pictured with small children could have been no more than thirty or thirty-five, but all looked aged. Everyone was underfed.

Lynn closed the album.

"I've seen this stuff before. It's my other life, yeah—the one I didn't have. Pretty awful. I've been deracinated, like zillions of people, but I'm *lucky* it happened, which makes me different. That's what you and mom think, right?"

"'Deracinated'?"

"Separated from my natural environment, my race, my native culture. My work at Columbia is kind of about that, how people and their families cope with it in old age." Leo squinted and nodded, then covered his eyes and tilted his head downward, concentrating now on something difficult.

"Whatever you say, sweetie…. Listen. While you're here I want to tell you something I never could before: *this was your mother's idea.*"

"I heard you tell Connie that this morning. I was downstairs. You didn't know."

He shook his head.

"I'm not talking about the charges against us. I mean your adoption…I didn't think we could do it—bring up another child, especially one from another race and culture. But your mother always did what she wanted, even if that involved driving her family off a cliff. You can't reason with her…So what I'm saying is, I was opposed to adopting you. I felt I had to tell you that. I can't say exactly why."

"It would have been better if you'd left me there? That's what you mean?"

"For you? Maybe. Who can say for sure what would have happened? I know that we gave you a nice roof over your head and a good education, which we can't do any longer. But I feel there should have been a lot more. For your mother and me? Well, *yes.* Without another child, we'd have gone our separate ways."

Leo was tearful.

"Dad—"

He held up his hand.

"None of this means I haven't cared for you. But I'm ashamed of what I've *been* for you. And I feel guilty about inflicting your mother on you. And now time's run out."

She gave him time to compose himself before saying, "Prison's definite?"

"Unless they're bluffing, yes. They say if I plead guilty, I might get easy time, a minimum-security place. Their concern is money. They want me putting every minute I have now into liquidating our assets. The better I do, the more lenient they'll be in their sentencing recommendation.

They know they won't be able to work with your mother."

"What'll they do to her?"

"I don't know or care…I *do* care, but I can't think about it. I've got to get through the next few weeks."

Both stared into space, past each other. In a corner, Lynn noticed the celadon elephant whose trunk she'd broken as a child. There had been a big scene afterward, her mother screaming. Lina had glued it, sloppily, insisting on keeping it out, in full view—as a reminder, Lynn felt, of something unspecified but humiliating.

"What about the dogs? Where'll they go?"

"Nick didn't want them. I knew you couldn't take them. So I dealt with it."

"There were here this morning. I saw them."

"The situation's been taken care of since then. You never know what you're capable of until you're forced to do it."

"You mean go to prison?"

"No. You asked about the dogs."

"I don't understand."

"I put them down."

" 'Put them down'? *Euthanized* them?"

"You can call it that. They're gone. I was going to break their necks, but my arthritis has been bothering me and my hands wouldn't have been up to it. I shot them."

"You *shot* them? You never owned a gun."

"I do now. I got it a few months ago, a little handgun. It's easier to use than I thought it would be. I hate to say this, but I like it, how it fits in my hand."

Later that day, Nick phoned. He asked about the dogs, where they'd go now, but without genuine interest. He had something to tell her.

"Dad killed them—shot them," Lynn said.

She sat at the desk in her old bedroom, on the second floor in front, overlooking the driveway, the cars, and—in an oval patch of lawn watered by a forty-two-thousand dollar irrigation system—a brilliant red paperbark maple. It was late afternoon. She was alone. Her father was in Palo Alto meeting lawyers.

Nick coughed to suppress a belch. He cleared his throat.

" 'Scuse me. Just had a huge dinner with the PDQ Telecom guys—they're ones we decided to underwrite. *Amazing* food, three-hundred-dollar wines…That's really too bad, about the pooches. I didn't know dad had a gun. I got one, too. The machete I had in Philly wouldn't cut it in New York."

Which was intended to be funny. She didn't respond.

"I called to say I'm not going to make it out there, after all."

The desk light shone in Lynn's eyes. She put her free hand to her forehead.

"Me and another rookie broker—guy I can't fucking stand, *huge* suck-up—we're invited to one of the vice president's homes in the Hamptons. No way can I finesse my way out of it if *he's* going. I'll be in touch with you and dad, and call mom."

"They're getting divorced."

"Oh…really?"

"Dad told me today."

She heard Nick breathing, absorbing the information.

"Don't mean to sound cold, but do we care?"

"I'm not sure how I feel about it. Though you'd think—"

"Might be part of some legal strategy," her brother interrupted, "so one of them can testify against the other and cut a deal with the D.A. Maybe dad's criminal lawyer advised him to do it. Husbands and wives can't be forced to nail each other in court. Turns out when there's a financial scam, the people pulling it off aren't sleaze bags, typically—they're a husband and wife, they've got a house, kids, the whole shebang."

"You sound like mom on speed."

"Whoa, Ragsie. That's nasty. *Like mom?*"

"Yeah, but faster. Maybe a little more understandable."

"Ouch! I didn't *hear* that…Hey, Ragsie, aren't you forgetting mom's upsides? One was saving your little butt from the human dung heap."

Without saying another word, Lynn hung up.

On her desk and the low bookcase beside it were things she'd grown up with, all dust-covered and forlorn-looking: a red-faced plastic Monkey King mask with sheaves of grain sprouting from its head; a nose-less, pigtailed "Chinese Dolly," bought by Lina in San Francisco's Chinatown; a bamboo drum with a fish-skin head; a K'ung chung, the spinning-top-and-string thing she never could work but Nick and his friends had mastered; a toy cart with tiny clay figures meant to represent the omnibus rigs that carried passengers between gates of the Imperial City in Beijing; and the duck rattle abandoned with her at the foundling home in Wuhan.

Lynn lifted the rattle and shook it. She'd always loved the natural, breathy sound the tiny pebbles inside made, like a light downpour of rain.

She picked up the waste basket beneath her desk and, with one arm, swept everything into it, then dropped to her knees, looking for the electrical outlet and phone jack she knew were there. The floor was covered with dust devils and the baseboard was lightly speckled with mold. She plugged in the laptop, turned it on, called up her e-mail.

Judy Frank was dead.

"I regret to inform the faculty, students, and staff of the Columbia University School of Social Work that Dr. Judith Miriam Frank passed away last night," the department chair had written. "She was seventy-one. A preliminary medical report indicated a massive stroke. Dr. Frank, a native of Augsburg, Germany, was one of the nation's leading social-welfare scholars, and the author of 'From Belarussia to Brighton: A Chronicle of Deracination, Diaspora, and Re-assimilation' (Oxford University Press, 1987), for which she was awarded the 1988 Thayer-Taubman Prize. Dr. Frank had been on the Columbia faculty since 1974. She taught previously at..."

The e-mail, probably a version of the statement going to the newspapers, went on to say that arrangements were being made to reassign Frank's graduate supervisees.

A car came up the driveway—Leo, back from the city. It passed the house, gravel flying up into the underbody. The garage opened, the car went in, the garage shut.

Her eyes fell to the waste basket. The duck, atop the pile of discarded toys, returned her gaze, mournfully. She thrust her hand into the basket and rescued it. She rose and carried it to the bed in open hands, like a newborn, set it down, lifted a sweater from her overnight bag, wrapped it, and placed it inside, carefully, so it wouldn't move when the carry-on was handled.

Outside there was a muffled crack—a branch breaking, she hoped, though the day had been windless.

She'd take the bag and the black boiled wool jacket she'd bought on Houston Street and leave now, walking to town, not looking left or right, not stopping. She'd call a cab at Ida's. By tomorrow she'd be home, and the day after inside the Lotus Blossom Nursing Inn, holding Mrs. Wing's and Jimmy Chan's hands.

She'd bring the duck rattle. It might delight them, wherever they were now, mentally, and it might not. Thinking it possibly would, in any case, was a comfort. She allowed herself to luxuriate in it, like mom at a spa, on a massage table, in a sea of almond lotion.

❧ *Prisoners of War* ❧

MARK WISNIEWSKI

You could say the turtle farm began the November I found a baby snapper on the street in front of my parents' house. It didn't make sense that he was there, especially then: every snapper I'd ever seen had been in water, and even I knew that, by November, they're supposed to be hibernating. Still, he was there, only the size of a half dollar and trying to cross the street, and I snatched him up to save him from getting run over, and then came the question of what to do with him. I could have taken him to O'Neill's Pond so he could dig himself into a hole there, but O'Neill's Pond was already iced over, so I took him into the house, where I ran the faucet in the kitchen sink and adjusted the temperature so it wouldn't shock him, then held him under the flow to remove the mud caked over his eyes. An eye finally opened, which I took as a sign that my brother would come home, but then again came the question of what to do with him.

I should probably explain that my brother was classified as "M.I.A.-presumed-P.O.W.," which still sometimes felt like luck because there was always the chance that he would come home fine. But the questions that seemed worth asking that day, rather than any about my brother, had to do with the baby snapper. Why was he that small in November? Could he have hatched so late? Why, when I held my finger in front of his mouth, didn't he snap at me?

Then I realized I could have stood in the kitchen thinking questions about him all day. If my parents came home and found me doing this, they would've told me to get rid of him and reminded me that the reason I needed G.E.D. was I didn't know when to stop asking questions in favor of acting how my years said I should. There was nothing wrong with my brain, my parents said. I just didn't apply myself was the problem. And applying myself, they said, meant *answering* the right questions rather than asking the kinds that made me wonder.

So I answered the question about what to do with the baby snapper by deciding he'd spend the winter in the sandbox in our back yard. It was a homemade sandbox, built out of pine planks by my father long before the first November he talked up enough votes to be Town Judge. My brother and I had played in it, but I knew better than to remember those days except to tell myself that some of the sand we'd played in was still there. There was also mud in there, which made me wonder how mud got past the wooden planks and here and there *over* the sand, but I knew this was one of those questions not worth asking when there was something I needed to do: help the baby snapper hibernate.

To help him, I decided, I'd bury him. So I took him out there, then buried him and worried he wouldn't be able to breathe. Shouldn't he bury *himself* might have been a question worth asking. And shouldn't he have some *water*. I decided to run to the basement and get the stationary tub my mother no longer used, and I did exactly that. How would he climb in was maybe a good question, so I let my thoughts answer it, then ran to the garage—where my raccoon hissed at me—and found a shovel. Why I still had that raccoon was certainly *not* a good question right then, and, back in the sandbox, I dug a hole wide enough for the stationary tub and deep enough that, after I packed sand and mud up to the lip of the tub, the baby snapper could climb in if he wanted. Then I jogged to the hose but saw it was already gone for the winter, probably onto the rafters in the garage, and I ran into the house and down into the basement and fetched our blue plastic cleaning pail and filled it with water I dumped into the stationary tub, then ran and filled and dumped again and again until the tub was full.

There, I thought as I caught my breath. I had run the whole time because my parents could have always come home. Then I saw The Clown walking down the alley toward me. The Clown was The Clown because he had a head that was bald on top but shaggy on the sides like many clowns you see. He was also odd, my parents said. He lived past the Town Line, in a house that had been abandoned after a fire had blackened its insides and eaten most of its roof, and he'd nailed up a new roof by himself, but it was plasterboard, which my mother said *proved* he was odd. Plus he was too poor to put shingles on the roof because the only job he could get was hauling large items the garbagemen wouldn't take. MAN WITH A VAN, the front of his van said, which even I knew was one of those things that, when you saw him driving toward you, was so obvious you didn't need to read about it.

Plus back when I'd been in school, kids in my classes had made fun of him because he hadn't gone to the war with our brothers because the military had said he was goofy, and in this town, when the military says something, you believe it, since most of us owe the food we've eaten and the roofs over our heads to paychecks from the army, the navy, the air force, or the marines. My father had been in the marines, and the time he'd spent there, he always said, was why he'd been voted Town Judge, so as much as I didn't like the marines because their commanders hadn't taken care of my brother the way I had when my brother was a kid following me around, I was never supposed to ask why any marines did what they did.

Anyway now those kids I'd been in school with were no longer my friends, because I'd failed too many tests and been held back too often, and because everyone else's brother but mine had come home dead or alive to a parade and maybe TV reporters in their yards, and no kid in town, it seemed, liked to be around me because of it, and he, The Clown, was now walking toward me. Why they didn't like to be around me was *not* a question to ask right then, especially after The Clown asked, "How's the raccoon?"

"What's it to you?" I said, which made me wonder how many townsfolk knew I had a raccoon, though the better question might have been why The Clown had talked to me when he hardly ever talked to anyone period. In fact, before I'd buried the stationary tub, he'd talked to me only once in my twenty-two years, maybe ten summers earlier, to ask how the trout were biting in O'Neill's Pond, and that was probably only because I'd surprised him by being in the troutiest gap in the shoreline brush after he'd walked past hundreds of thorns to get there.

"Just curious is all," he said now, and he stopped in his tracks. He was right there, out in the alley.

"Don't ask what I'm doing here, cause I'll tell you," I said. "Found a baby snapper in the road out front. Making sure he hibernates right."

"In a sandbox."

"More of a turtle farm now," I said, and I had to admit I now liked talking to The Clown, because it had caused me to think up the idea of a turtle farm right then and there. The following summer, there would be as many turtles as I could catch in that farm, to keep the baby snapper company if he survived the winter.

"I helped your pa build that sandbox, you know," he said.

"Can't say I did," I said.

"When you was maybe five," he said.

"Seems I'd remember that if it were true," I said.

"You was in the house with a cold," he said. "Smack in the middle of the summer, and your pa said you was coughing up green."

There he'd mentioned an actual fact, so I believed him about helping with the sandbox.

He nodded. "You want more turtles, stop by my house next spring. Got a rowboat now. Plenty of snappers out in those lily pads toward the middle of O'Neill's Pond."

"I'll consider it, thanks," I said, though his far-away look had me sure we would never talk again.

"Know which house is mine?" he asked.

"The one with no shingles."

"You could say that," he said, and I could tell by how his face went sour that he wanted to ask how I knew where he lived but that he just as well knew that question wasn't worth asking, and he turned to walk off. When his back was completely to me, he stopped to face me without really facing me. "You or your folks need rubbish removed," he said, "I'll do it for cheap. I got a reliable van."

"Sure enough," I said, and again he walked on, and here I was sitting in a rotting sandbox with a baby snapper I suddenly couldn't see. *He's already dug in?* I thought, and even before I decided whether that question was worth applying myself to, I heard my father's car door slam out front, and I hustled buns into the house so he wouldn't see me sitting on muddy sand and ask what in heck I was doing.

🦋 🦋

But I'll tell you, there was nothing that felt more noble that winter than how, come spring, I'd have what you'd call a turtle farm. Sure my G.E.D. was the goal I was supposed to concentrate on, because with a G.E.D. I could get a job that would allow me to support myself as an adult my age was supposed to, but I couldn't say any adults I knew of with jobs, whether they were my age or not, seemed to have what my mother said I lacked: self-es*teem*. If you listened to my father when he returned from a day as Town Judge, the average adult with a job around here also had a divorce or a property dispute or a DUI or an assault charge, which didn't sound like the kinds of things that would have made me feel good about myself, or anyone else for that matter. But a *turtle farm*? That made me feel good even when so much snow covered our back yard you could barely believe a sandbox was out there. It would be its own world, complete with a pond that wouldn't look like a stationary tub if I covered its lip with rocks in case the mud over the lip was washed away by rain, and there could be wild flowers planted by wind, and if I stayed quiet enough, butterflies might land. If it looked as good as I imagined and I caught enough turtles, I could charge neighbor kids to see it, and maybe word of it would spread to the Chamber of Commerce and Triple-A, and people driving past town on vacations would pay to see and photograph it. Maybe they'd pay enough that I'd never need to work for anyone else, and then I'd be employed by my own world, one I'd invented in my mind only because my eyes had been down when I'd walked across the street and seen that all-but-dry baby snapper.

At some time that winter, the question about why I had my raccoon seemed to be one I was supposed to ask, because my parents kept asking it. Maybe they were asking because the raccoon, which still didn't have a name because no name would stick to it, was getting wilder than ever, screaming his raccoon scream whenever I walked inside the garage to feed him or my father pulled his Electra in there to park, and scratching and gnawing at the corners of the plywood-and-quarter-inch-screen cage I'd built after I'd rescued him from the chimney above the fireplace my parents were too busy to use. You'd think a young raccoon stuck in a chimney because its mother had become road kill would take to the body who'd lowered clothesline sewn to an old pillow case to bring it up to the roof where it could see the real world, but when I finally got this guy into the pillow case and hauled him to freedom, he didn't exactly nuzzle me. He did let me hold him, but he was shaking and hissing and now and then chomping on my hand. A book I read for my G.E.D. said raccoons make forty-five different noises, one of them like a cat's purr, but I didn't hear anything of that sort from this guy, though as I built his cage, he did follow me around like my brother used to, and he did eat the dog food I gave him and stand and chirp for breakfast when I walked into the garage most mornings.

As that winter went on, though, he'd taken to hissing through his snout more often and even growling now and again, and he was getting bigger by the day, huge even, to the point that, when I'd clean his cage, I'd put scrap plywood over the hole that normally let him go from one floor of his pen to other—so he wouldn't bite me while I cleaned the floor he wasn't on. Sometimes, as I'd clean his cage, I wondered if, since he'd once followed me around like my brother had, my parents wanted me to let him go so it would be easier for them to imagine my brother being let out of some P.O.W cage overseas, and when I'd wonder that, I'd want to let the raccoon go, too. Then he'd usually calm down some, as if the part of him that still wasn't wild had talked the rest of him into behaving like a puppy, and I'd think that, if my parents still believed I could get a G.E.D., I should be able to believe I could have a raccoon I could walk with a leash someday.

Then, toward the end of that winter, our refrigerator broke. Actually it still put out cold air, but it froze what it was supposed to chill and didn't freeze what it was supposed to keep frozen to the point that my parents began arguing. Anyway they could either pay some money from their savings to get it fixed, or pay more of it to buy a new one, which would mean the old one would have to go because there was no room for it in the garage—especially seeing I'd built the raccoon's cage in there—and this was a problem since the town laws my father enforced allowed Large Item Pick-Up only two days a year, one at the beginning and one at the end of each summer, and there was no way, my mother said, that two refrigerators and three people could stay in the house until June. As my parents were having these arguments, which included whispers about The Clown, I kept wondering about The Clown, because I just knew that somehow, no matter what came of our sort-of-broken refrigerator, either my mother or my father would remember the words MAN WITH A VAN and think to pay The Clown to haul it away, and I didn't want that to happen because, if The Clown came over, he might ask them about the turtle farm, and then they'd ask *me* about the turtle farm. Which would mean I could either lie to keep alive my dream about the farm, or tell the truth, in which case they might say I couldn't have the farm because turtles would distract me from getting my G.E.D., especially since I already had a raccoon. And I didn't want to lie, because if I would, I would lose *honor*, which my father said was the one thing I could always share with my brother the marine whether or not he'd come home.

And sure as the sun sets, my father phoned The Clown, and that afternoon the words MAN WITH A VAN appeared in front our house, stopping right where I'd found the baby snapper, and I wanted to hide so the sight of me wouldn't cause The Clown even to *think* a question about the turtle farm, but if I hid and he asked my parents about it, I wouldn't be there to change the subject, so I grabbed an apple from the wooden bowl on the counter and a knife from the knife box and sat at the kitchen table as he walked his dolly in, then took my time peeling the apple to keep our eyes from meeting as he earned my parents' cash. And the peeling excuse worked as he strapped up the old refrigerator and wheeled it out. Then he came back to collect his cash, and after he had it and my parents thanked him and said their goodbyes, I heard the words "Still plannin' a turtle farm?" and got pissed as the dickens, because it didn't seem fair that, after all of those minutes peeling, I'd had to fail at the very *end* of The Clown's only time ever in our house.

And if I didn't answer right off, my silence would bring that much more attention to me, so I blurted, "I got all sorts of plans."

"I still got that rowboat," he said, and as much as I knew his words would raise all sorts of questions in my parents' minds, I had to admit the thought of netting turtles out of O'Neill's Pond was one I wanted to keep, even if it meant sitting in a boat with The Clown. Then he slid my parents' cash into his flannel pocket, and he was gone, and all I could do was eat my apple.

"What did he mean, 'turtle farm'?" my father asked in his Town Judge sort of way, and my mind pictured a single word: *honor*.

"Just a guy talking, I guess," I said.

"Yeah, but he was talking to you," my mother said. "About a *turtle* farm."

"Seems he's just what we always thought he was," I said. "You know, odd."

🐉 🐉

For the rest of that winter I wondered if I'd lost honor by saying what I'd said about The Clown, because if that were true and all my brother had left was his own honor, I might have weakened the last tie between us. I tried to think that maybe, long before I'd mentioned my turtle farm to The Clown in the first place, my brother had told whoever might have captured him more than his name, rank, and serial number, and that maybe, as a result, he was no longer a P.O.W., just a man who'd decided honor wasn't worth all the torture he faced, especially when, without honor, he might have been let out of his cage, where he could walk and eat and maybe see turtles among lily pads on some overseas lagoon that looked like O'Neill's Pond. Maybe he was free and, wherever he was, living with a wife as most men of his years did, and maybe his future there would be more like a dream than it would have been here. I knew it wasn't good to think about such a life for him, because when I had asked my parents about him living such a life, they'd told me that was the *precise* kind of question I was never supposed to ask, but I liked thinking about it anyway. Maybe he felt like a turtle in my farm would feel if my farm turned out as I imagined it.

Then, finally, spring began to itch, and I kept finding myself at the rear window of our house, gazing out at the snow in the sandbox as if the heat from my eyes could help it melt. I still hadn't worked out in my mind how I'd convince my parents that a turtle farm was worth the effort for a man of my age. Anyway it might hurt the baby snapper, I thought, to rush it out of hibernation too early, so I tried to be patient about the snow, which took weeks to melt in the corners of the sandbox because it was more or less ice there. Then, one day, every bit of snow and ice was gone, and from then on, whenever I was home alone, I took to standing beside the sandbox with my arms folded, waiting to see the baby snapper undig itself. Of course I wanted to see his face again, but I was also curious about questions like whether turtles grow at all while they hibernate—because it didn't seem fair that a body couldn't grow at all during half of every year, which would altogether mean half of its life. And I couldn't say how many times I stood outside staring at that muddy sand. Sometimes I'd think I'd see a grain of it move, but then I'd kneel and know my imagination had seen what my eyes hadn't, and I'd feel ornery inside, not as pissed as I'd felt when The Clown's question in the kitchen had put me in that fix, but sure close to it, because I was smart enough to know that if I had to dig up the baby snapper rather than see him dig himself out, chances were I'd be pulling him out of his grave. Plus, if he'd just poke his head out of that sand, probably all but the laziest turtles that had hibernated in O'Neill's Pond were on their way to swimming toward new lily pads, where I could catch them and show them an even better life in my farm.

Then came the moment that a grain *actually* moved, and here's the snapper's tail, swishing clumps of mud out of its way: the little bastard was coming out rear-first, and I was so happy at the sight, I would have cried if I hadn't been thinking, just before he appeared, about how I would have to behave up to my years when it came to the turtle farm—to convince my parents to allow me to have it. I also wanted to help him out to rush time toward the sight of his face, but not to help would be good practice for how I'd make the farm as natural a place for turtles as any. Then he was all clear of the muddy sand. If he were any bigger than in November, it wasn't by more than a tiny fraction, and I figured holding him for a few seconds was only fair because I, after all, was the body who'd saved his life. So that's what I did, close to my face. Both of his eyes were open, and he seemed maybe as sluggish as when I'd found him but brighter when it came to how he looked at the world. I set him back down, and he walked over sand and mud and plopped himself in the tub, where he sunk, then floated with his legs stuck out, and where, after I counted to forty-six, he finally blinked.

Then brakes squeaked in the alley, which might have meant my father was home but then, the more I asked myself what time it was, probably meant something not deserving that much worry, and I mustered the courage to look up and see it again, MAN WITH A VAN.

"Anytime you want to come over," The Clown said through his rolled-down window, "we can net you some turtles."

"I'll consider it, thanks," I said, and he looked at me as if he thought I were as odd as townsfolk thought he was, then nodded at me and drove off.

❧ ❦

The Clown's garbage cans didn't have covers, and his door was open, and a potbellied dog walked out from inside and sniffed my hands gently, like I wished my raccoon would. I asked myself the question I'm supposed to ask when I get nervous and feel lost: Why am I here? I could smell O'Neill's Pond, which I'd never thought could have lapped up onto The Clown's property, and all at once I *knew* why The Clown didn't mind having a house without shingles: he could walk right out of his open doorway and over a path through woods and sit beside water full of trout and turtles—and therefore feel like the king of the world. If that were true, it was a good life he had, or at least one that smelled so good it didn't matter if his walls were still burnt. Then he, The Clown himself, poked his head out his doorway and waved me inside, where I saw that only one of his walls was still black. Other than the plasterboard roof, he didn't have a ceiling, which meant coaxial cable and wires snaked from rafters to light the only two bulbs he used, and he had a cot he didn't mind mussed, and there, in the far corner of the house, which was all one room, was my parents' old refrigerator—or one that looked darned like it.

"Have a beer?" he asked.

"Sure," I said even though, when I'd been eighteen, my parents had said beer was why I'd failed classes in high school. He opened the refrigerator, snatched a bottle, and handed it over, and the beer tasted good in that way something bad for you tastes, and its coldness told me that the refrigerator, whoever it once belonged to, was now fine. Then he and I stood facing each other, and I would have asked a question to be polite, but it seemed beer was the answer to any question in that house. And this beer, with a label I'd never seen, had kick to it. Someday another house might burn, I thought, and I might live like this, too. In the meantime, I again asked myself why I was there: the turtle farm.

"The baby snapper's fine," I said. "I mean, the one I found last fall."

"Good," The Clown said. "Let's get him some company." He reached behind a stained couch with three different-sized cushions and pulled out a landing net, and I began for his doorway, where the potbellied dog nudged me into petting behind its ears, then followed me past pine trees between the house and O'Neill's Pond, and I felt too alone, as if The Clown had disappeared. When I turned around, though, he was behind me, but well behind me, and any question about his distance was answered by the ten or so beers in the landing net. He caught up to me on the muddy part of the shoreline where his boat sat. Aluminum oars were soldered into its oar locks, and he got in the boat, which didn't have life cushions, then looked out over the water and opened a beer, and I couldn't wait to catch turtles but wanted a cushion, which my parents had said my brother and I needed whenever we were on boats—and he faced me with this cranky frown and said, "Something wrong?"

"You don't have life cushions," I said.

"Them's for kids," he said, and I laughed some worry from me and got in the boat myself. It sat lower in the water than you'd think, and he handed me an open beer, and I sipped as he shoved us off, and then we were out there, on O'Neill's Pond, which looks bigger when you're on it than it does from shore. The sun escaped from behind a cloud, and I felt as good as I could remember feeling, so good I forgot what we had set out to do, but The Clown rowed as if he'd always know why he was rowing, in charge of the world almost. It was like he and I were men and boys at the same time, and I kept thinking about how, as odd as we might have been considered on the other side of the Town Line, we were where we belonged. If only the turtle farm could feel like this, I thought. For the turtles *and* me. Then he said, "There" in this flat way that still couldn't hide how he loved to see a turtle poke out of water, and I could tell by his eyes where this particular one was, the yellow-striped head of a painter beside lily pads that had growing to do. That turtle disappeared and never re-surfaced, but soon another head popped up to breathe, then another and another, most of them painters, and one key to catching them was for The Clown to row hard once or twice toward them, then *glide* until they saw us and dove a foot underwater believing they were safe when they weren't. I was in charge of netting, and another key was to scoop *lower* than you figured you should, and before long, time felt like nothing but sunshine and lily pads and turtles crawling over the empties we'd set under our seats to keep O'Neill's Pond from being polluted. We were a team, The Clown and I, and it didn't feel exactly like being with a brother, but it was as close to that feeling as I'd had since the day my brother left for the war. We caught more turtles than we missed; I was happy even after the beer had thinned out on my insides. I didn't think it best to ask The Clown if he were happy, but the more turtles we captured, the less I thought of him as odd.

When we got back to shore, though, he all at once acted as if he couldn't talk, and he followed the potbellied dog into their house as I gathered the caught turtles into the landing net—there were eight. He returned with two beers in his hand, gave me one, and gulped down the other with the shade of a pine tree on his face. He said, "Any time you want to catch more, I'll go with you." He glanced toward his van. "Let me get you a box," he said. He swigged foam, then moseyed toward his van, then untied rope that kept its dented rear doors shut. He pulled out a box and stood holding it—maybe to decide how strong it was? Or was he remembering something, maybe something about my brother, or some distant brother of his own? Finally he brought the box over to me and said "Here," and that was the last word between us.

🐢 🐢

Of course my parents noticed the turtles, but it took them almost a week, maybe because the sandbox was one of those things they figured was no longer worth their attention. And I doubt they'd have noticed the turtles if I hadn't spent all that time outside. I would stand beside the sandbox and watch turtles swim and sunbathe. Sometimes one would try to escape only to learn its claws couldn't reach the top of a pine wall, or two would sleep side-by-side in the sunshine, or one would sleep beside a wall and another would climb on the sleeping one's shell, only to get closer to the top, then fall and land on its back, then struggle to right itself.

It was just after a turtle had righted itself on a gray morning that my mother appeared beside me and said, "I'll be darned."

"From O'Neill's Pond," I said, to stop her from having to ask a question. Then, so there would be no questions at all, I went ahead and told her: "The Clown helped me catch them."

"As in, 'Man with a Van'?"

I nodded. "I call this a turtle farm."

"You feed them from the fridge?" she asked.

Which, to me, meant she was digging for reasons for me to give up the farm: in my father's eyes, groceries were expensive even though he'd been Town Judge for years. So I said, "No. I figure they eat worms."

"In a *sand*box?"

"There's mud in there."

"Yes," she said. "But have you *seen* any worms?"

Here's where I could have lied to save my farm, but I didn't want to, because I'd already dodged the truth when The Clown had stood in our kitchen and, if I had any honor left to share with my brother, I didn't want to spend the very last of it. So I said, "No," and she walked off and disappeared into the house, where I believed she was phoning my father to begin the part of my life that would end with all of my turtles back in O'Neill's. Will they prefer it there? I wondered. Will they remember the stationary tub?

Then the back door opened and she returned, and I got so nervous I had to ask myself *twice* why we were there before I remembered what had seemed about to happen. But she didn't say anything, just tossed a piece of olive loaf into the stationary tub, then toed the little snapper from the edge of the tub into the water. He sunk and stayed down there, then saw the olive loaf, eased closer to it, sized it up, stretched his neck, and *chomped* a hole in it shaped like his jaw. My brother had always liked olive loaf, and I wondered if asking my mother if she remembered this would cause her to want to keep the farm for *her*, but then I told myself to keep my thoughts about him silent right then, which was probably what he would have preferred had he known what we were doing.

"It's cute," she said. "I mean, the way he gobbled it down."

"So I can keep the farm?"

"I'd say yes. But of course, there's your father."

❧ ❧

My father's decision, which he announced after a nap, was that I could keep every turtle if I let my raccoon go. To have both the raccoon and the farm would "tax my concentration," he said, and I knew he was glad because, in his mind, the raccoon had kept me from getting my G.E.D. He also said that, to keep the farm, I had to promise never to visit The Clown again, and then he and my mother explained that my father himself had judged a trial about whether The Clown had made love to a teenage girl. They took their time to explain this, as if I didn't know that people make love even though my father had explained that to me while I'd gapped spark plugs for him ten years earlier, and also as if I didn't know it was wrong for a man to make love to a girl who was in high school, which is one of those things you learn in *middle* school just from hearing students talk. The trial had found The Clown innocent, but my father explained that this verdict was only because a young lawyer had wanted to show off what *he'd* learned in school, and I couldn't tell who my father disliked more, the lawyer or The Clown, but no matter: if I'd keep the farm, my time with both The Clown and my raccoon were over.

Letting the raccoon go bothered me mostly because to open his cage and watch him gallop out of the garage and up the alley meant I'd never tame him, but now that I had the turtles, I knew I'd tried to tame him only to prove to myself that niceness, including my brother's, could defeat any mean streak, including the mean streaks of any overseas soldiers who might have put him in a cage. As for turning my back on The Clown, this also bothered me some, because I'd hoped to net turtles with him on at least one more of those sunny weekdays, but I convinced myself that what we'd caught plus the little snapper were enough that they might reproduce, then concentrated on making their world pleasant for them. I covered the edge of the stationary tub with slices of blue shale and limestone, one then the other all the way around, and draped them with transplanted lime-green creepers I'd spooned out of cracks between sidewalks, and found a fat, moss-covered log I propped with a red rock to create shade. I planted sugar maple saplings I would prune to look like trees. I couldn't stand to wait for the wind to plant wild flowers, so, at the hardware store, I bought a seed packet with a picture of probably every kind of wild flower on it. And I'll be darned if tiny sprouts didn't appear, and at least two dozen survived despite the flattening they'd take as the turtles walked over them, and cabbage butterflies and viceroys and black and yellow swallowtails landed, and people who saw the farm said they'd pay to see it again.

But I never charged anyone. Though as soon as word about the farm got around, nearly every kid within the town lines and even some adults asked onto our property to lay eyes on it, and, after I'd let them, they'd stand with grins smacked onto their faces, so I knew I'd done something more magic than getting a G.E.D. It was a place of beauty, I'll tell you, sort of a country of its own, where turtles were turtles and anger could never belong. Just after the Fourth of July, it troubled me that The Clown would never see it, but if I knew The Clown, he'd check it out some night with a flashlight. God bless The Clown, I'd think when I'd wake before dawn and wonder if he were out there.

Then, after Labor Day, when more people saw my turtles than ever in one day, the summer slid into that quickness anything good takes on toward its end, and even though townsfolk still visited and asked about the farm, the only questions I allowed in my mind concerned how well the little snapper—which had grown more—would hibernate. Would he wait until November again? What if a bigger turtle dug him up? And what about springtime? Would he make his way out? Would people still want to see him? So many questions about hibernation came into my head as September moved past, I had trouble remembering the meanings of even three-letter words in the books I was supposed to read to get my G.E.D.

Then October arrived, and, one by one, the turtles dug past elm leaves that had landed on the sandy mud, as if olive loaf and sunshine no longer mattered, as if the only question in any turtle's mind was how fast it could hide. Only the little snapper seemed to want to enjoy the farm as long as he could, but then, two days before Halloween, even he worked his way down. He wasn't completely gone until the third day of November, when the end of his tail disappeared. Okay, I thought. Everyone's set to live here next spring.

But that was the thing about November of that year. It was the one when something in me, whenever I looked down on the farm, wondered how it would be to know that my brother would never come back. There would be no parade planned to stop at our house. There would be no reporters in our yard. There would only be a sandbox full of leaves and sand and mud—and turtles who once tried to return to where they'd been born, sometimes alone, sometimes by standing on each other's backs, but always, always failing.

❧ *Acknowledgments* ❧

"Enoch Arden's One Night Stands" appeared several years ago in the *Beloit Fiction Journal.*

"Hideous Thing" was named third-place winner in the 2006 Summer Literary Seminars fiction competition, judged by Margaret Atwood.

"Jasmine, Washing the Hair of Pearsa" appeared in *Indiana Review.*

"Prisoners of War" appeared in *Glimmer Train.*

"The Mean" appeared in *Best New American Voices.*

Thanks to the editors of these journals.

❧ *Contributors' Bios* ❧

JACOB M. APPEL's short fiction has appeared in *Agni, Bellevue Literary Review, Greensboro Review, Southwest Review, StoryQuarterly,* and elsewhere. He holds an MFA from New York University, and has most recently taught at Brown University in Providence, Rhode Island, and the Gotham Writers' Workshop in New York City. Jacob can be found on the Internet at www.jacobmappel.com and he welcomes email at jma38@columbia.edu.

STEPHENIE BROWN is working hard on a novel featuring Franklin Yancey, a character who appears in "The Wheelwright." She grew up in a small Alabama town, then traveled in distant parts of the world. She has a JD from Columbia Law School and a BA from the University of Alabama, where she studied Chinese and German. Until recently she was a partner at a New York law firm. She now lives in Virginia with a handsome Australian man, a brilliant baby boy, and a passionate Chihuahua. She enjoys writing wicked verse. This is her first published (and first submitted) story.

LAUREN COBB's fiction has appeared or is forthcoming in *Beloit Fiction Journal, Green Mountains Review, Eclipse, Jabberwock Review,* and other journals. Originally from Los Angeles, she now lives in northern Minnesota, where she's an Associate Professor of English at Bemidji State University. She has completed her first novel and is working on a short story collection.

GREG HRBEK is the author of a novel, *The Hindenburg Crashes Nightly.* His short fiction and non-fiction has appeared in *Harper's, Salmagundi, Idaho Review, Sonora Review,* and *The Bridport Prize Anthology 2006.* He lives with his wife and son in the Northern Mariana Islands, and teaches part of the year at Skidmore College in Upstate New York.

VALERIE HURLEY's fiction and essays have been published in *The Iowa Review, The Massachusetts Review, New Letters, Indiana Review, Boston Review, The Missouri Review,* and other magazines and anthologies. Four of her essays have been awarded "Most Notable" status in *Best American Essays*. Her first novel, *St. Ursula's Girls Against the Atomic Bomb*, was published by MacAdam/Cage in 2003 and by Plume Books (in paperback) in 2004. She has enjoyed residencies at the MacDowell Colony, the Millay Colony, and the Vermont Studio Center. She lives in northern Vermont with her playwright husband, John Kern, and feels very fortunate to be represented by literary agent Betsy Lerner of Dunow, Carlson & Lerner.

BENJAMIN NOAM PEARLBERG grew up in Toronto, Ontario and Southfield, Michigan. He has earned degrees at Columbia University and for the past four years has been studying in yeshiva. He currently lives in New York with his wife, Lisa.

MATTHEW PITT was born and raised in St. Louis. He received his BA at Hampshire College and his MFA at New York University, where he was a *New York Times* Fellow in Fiction. His fiction has appeared in numerous journals, such as *The Southern Review*, *Alaska Quarterly Review*, *Witness*, and *Colorado Review*. Work of his has also won awards or been honored by *Glimmer Train*, *Missouri Review*, *Inkwell*, the Salem College Center for Women Writers, the Bread Loaf Writers' Conference, and *Pushcart Prize XXX*.

SCOTT WINOKUR was a San Francisco Bay Area newspaperman for 29 years. He has won about 40 national, state and regional journalism awards, including the American Bar Association's Silver Gavel and the National Headliners Club award. For nearly seven years, he was a columnist for the (Hearst-owned) *San Francisco Examiner* and, for 11 years, an investigative and enterprise reporter for the *Examiner* and the *San Francisco Chronicle*. His freelance journalism has appeared in *Cosmopolitan*, *Redbook*, and other national publications. His profile of V.S. Naipaul was anthologized in *Conversations with V.S. Naipaul* (ed. Feroza Jussawalla, University Press of Mississippi, 1997).

MARK WISNIEWSKI is the author of the novel *Confessions of a Polish Used Car Salesman*. His stories are published or forthcoming in more than 100 magazines including *Triquarterly, Antioch Review, The Georgia Review, Boulevard, Glimmer Train, The Missouri Review, New England Review, The Sun, Fiction International, The Yale Review, Confrontation, Fiction, Indiana Review, Mississippi Review, American Short Fiction, Prism International,* and *Virginia Quarterly Review.* He's the recipient of a Pushcart Prize and the winner of the 2006 Tobias Wolff Award and a 2006 Isherwood Foundation Fellowship in Fiction.

DEL SOL PRESS, based out of Washington, D.C., publishes exemplary and edgy fiction, poetry, and nonfiction (mostly contemporary, with the occasional reprint). Founded in 2002, the press sponsors two annual competitions:

THE DEL SOL PRESS POETRY PRIZE is a yearly book-length competition with a January deadline for an unpublished book of poems.

THE ROBERT OLEN BUTLER FICTION PRIZE is awarded for the best short story, published or unpublished. The deadline is in November of each year.

http://webdelsol.com/DelSolPress

Printed in the United States
89198LV00004B/52/A

9 780979 150166